Jinxed!

The Curious Curse
of Cora Bell

Jinxed!
The Curious Curse
of Cora Bell

Rebecca McRitchie
illustrated by Sharon O'Connor

📖 Angus&Robertson
An imprint of HarperCollins*Children's Books*

Angus&Robertson
An imprint of HarperCollins*Children'sBooks*, Australia

First published in Australia in 2019
by HarperCollins*Publishers* Australia Pty Limited
ABN 36 009 913 517
harpercollins.com.au

HarperCollins*Publishers*
Level 13, 201 Elizabeth Street, Sydney NSW 2000, Australia
Unit D1, 63 Apollo Drive, Rosedale, Auckland 0632, New Zealand
A 53, Sector 57, Noida, UP, India
1 London Bridge Street, London SE1 9GF, United Kingdom
2 Bloor Street East, 20th floor, Toronto, Ontario M4W 1A8, Canada
195 Broadway, New York NY 10007, USA

A Catalogue record entry for this book is available
from the National Library of Australia

ISBN 978 1 4607 5764 2 (paperback)
ISBN 978 1 4607 1130 9 (ebook)

Cover design by Amy Daoud, HarperCollins Design Studio
Cover and internal illustrations by Sharon O'Connor
Typeset in Bembo Std by Kirby Jones
Printed and bound in Australia by McPherson's Printing Group
The papers used by HarperCollins in the manufacture of this book are
a natural, recyclable product made from wood grown in sustainable
plantation forests. The fibre source and manufacturing processes meet
recognised international environmental standards, and carry certification.

Prologue

The Princess in the Yellow Nightdress

In a crowded forest, not near anywhere, a woman in a yellow nightdress ran for her life. Her long, amber hair lashed behind her as she gasped heavy breaths and sprinted barefoot between the trees. Her back stung from where her wings once were. The remaining feathers fell away in tufts at her feet.

She stopped running when the ground ended. Panting, she looked out in front of her. Nothing but night filled the space as she peered over a high, rocky cliff.

There was a loud screech behind her and she whirled around to see a bolt of lightning ricochet against the trees. Then as quickly as it came, it disappeared, leaving only silence. She searched the dark forest and waited, her heart beating fast.

She looked for a glimmer, a ruffle. Something. Anything.

Then the sound of deep laughter filled the air.

'All alone, princess?' came a voice from the forest.

She felt her fear double in her chest. Without her wings, there wasn't much chance of escape. She knew that now. She took a deep breath and squared her bloodstained shoulders. With shaking hands, she called up the air around her until it was a swirling, roaring wind in her ears.

'Argh!' she cried as she hurled the wall of wind into the forest. Leaves flew from their branches, trees bent and snapped, and the ground shook. Then, without pause, she hurled another and another and another until the trees in front of her were bare. And standing still, amongst the trunks, was the dark silhouette of a man with long silver hair, gleaming eerily in the light from the moon.

Suddenly, a great gold bird burst from the trees. It flew towards her and grabbed her by the shoulders with its talons. The bird carried her off the ground in a large swoop until they were flying over the cliff.

'No, Artemis!'

There was another crack of lightning but this time it was followed by a sharp pain in her chest. The bird dipped in flight, injured. He struggled to hold her.

There wasn't much time. She looked up at her friend, tears in her eyes.

'Take it,' she breathed. She let go of what she had been holding onto for so long. Then she pulled the talons from her shoulders and fell, a flowing tangle of amber and yellow silently plummeting towards the ground.

Chapter One

In the city of Urt, there was a wall. It was tall and wide, like most walls. It was boring and plain, also like most walls. But unlike most walls, and unbeknownst to all, behind that wall in the city of Urt lived an elderly lady named Dot and a young girl named Cora.

Behind the wall, in the space where they lived, Cora awoke one morning to the sound of a lullaby floating into her room. The gentle music sounded like it was far away at first so the young girl turned over in her bed and tried to go back to sleep. When the music persisted, Cora woke with a jolt, and sat up, wide-awake.

'No, no, no,' she pleaded.

With a *whoosh*, Cora shoved her blanket away and jumped out of bed. She pushed aside clothes and hopped over the trinkets strewn by her feet on the floor. She threw on her favourite green dress.

Her mind still foggy with sleep, she tried to think. What else did she need? *Shoes!* She whirled around, searching for her boots. She found one on its side by the door and wrestled it on.

'Scratch! Where's my other shoe?!'

Scratch, the cat, yawned and stretched unhelpfully from his place on the bed.

Diving to her knees, Cora pushed aside her pile of books and grabbed her pack from beneath her bed. The pack she kept just for these situations. Throwing it on, she raced to the door and opened it, only to come face to face with Dot.

Crud.

The old lady stood with one hand behind her back and the other holding a shiny pocket watch. Her soft face was wrinkled in disappointment.

'Cora,' she said.

'I know,' Cora replied, looking down at her one-booted foot.

'Five whole minutes. Luckily this was only a drill. But what if it had been the real thing? The lullaby —'

'— means trouble,' Cora finished. 'I know.'

'Yes, it means trouble and *run*.' Dot sighed. 'How am I supposed to let you collect by yourself *out there*,' she gestured to the wall that sat between them and the city outside, 'when you take five whole minutes to run from fake trouble *in here*?'

Cora groaned. She knew Dot was right. Since they had started doing drills, Cora had failed every single one of them. When she heard the lullaby from Dot's gramophone, Cora was supposed to drop what she was doing, grab her pack and shoes, and meet Dot at the top of the wall as quickly as she could. But each time, Cora either went back to sleep, was too slow, forgot to grab her pack, or, like today, was missing one boot.

'Sorry,' Cora mumbled.

'Well,' Dot said, 'it doesn't help when you have a cat that likes to steal boots and eat them.'

Cora looked up to see Dot smiling.

'This was beneath the table,' Dot said. Then the old lady pulled out Cora's missing boot from behind her back. The purple laces were half-chewed.

'Scratch!' Cora cried. 'You pesky cat!'

Scratch purred from his place on the bed.

'C'mon,' Dot said with a chuckle. 'I made porridge.'

Cora hopped on one foot as she put on her missing boot and followed Dot into the main room.

The space behind the wall where they lived was small. In fact, it was even smaller than small because from ceiling to floor, much of the room was taken up by things. Vases, fishing rods, picture frames, lamps, books. Some were pieces and parts forgotten. Others were odds and ends purposefully left behind. Dot and Cora collected them all. Well, they scavenged them all. But Dot and Cora preferred to call it collecting and themselves collectors. They loved what they found. And every now and then they found something that others wanted too. Nobody suspected that the most successful scavengers in the city of Urt were an old lady and a young girl. But they were.

On the small, rickety, round table in the middle of the main room sat two bowls of porridge. Last week, Dot had traded one of her sewing kits for a jar of oats as a surprise. Cora didn't remember much before meeting Dot, but porridge had always been her favourite.

They sat and ate. The delicious, fluffy lumps warmed Cora up from her toes to her nose.

'There's a new job,' said Dot opposite her.

Cora looked up from her bowl.

'A trader from Mill Town is looking for something small.'

'When are we going?' Cora asked, scoffing the remains of her porridge.

'Not *we* this time, Cora,' Dot said. 'You.'

'Me?' Cora replied, almost choking on an oat. Her excitement evaporated.

Dot nodded.

Cora looked at the wall hesitantly. 'But what about …?' she couldn't bring herself to say it.

The old lady smiled warmly at her. 'You're not like others, Cora,' Dot said gently. 'But you're stronger than you think.'

Cora wasn't so sure about that.

'I'm not going to be around forever,' Dot added.

'Please don't,' said Cora softly. She didn't want to think about a time when Dot wouldn't be around. Instinctively, she grabbed the bracelet that hung from her wrist. Cora remembered when the old lady had found her five years ago. The bracelet and the clothes she wore were the only things she had. She remembered the feeling of coldness, of rain, of fear at the loss of her eye and the red, bumpy scar that sat in its place. Then she remembered looking up at Dot's kind face, and it all going away.

Dot reached over and placed a hand on Cora's. 'It's time,' she said.

Although butterflies had now entered her stomach, Cora found herself nodding.

Dot gave her a proud smile before standing up from the table. The old lady walked over to the bookshelf in the corner of the room crammed full with heavy, bound books and old newspapers. She shuffled through the pages of a newspaper, walked back and placed a page on the table in front of Cora.

'You are looking for this,' she said, pointing to a drawing. Cora looked down at it, memorising every line, every stroke and every letter with her eye.

'Toe Tippins Shoe Polish.'

Chapter Two

After saying goodbye to Dot and Scratch, Cora climbed the ladder down from the wall. When she reached the bottom, she stood for a moment in the narrow alleyway. Looking down it, she could see the smoke from the metal factory, the grey sky and the shadows of people moving about at the other end.

Cora took a deep breath to settle the fear that wriggled uncomfortably in her stomach. She always walked the city with Dot. In the rougher and darker parts, sometimes she would even hold Dot's hand. Nervously, Cora grabbed the bracelet that hung from her wrist.

'You can do this,' she whispered to herself. Then, squaring her shoulders, she stepped forward and kept stepping forward until she reached the end of the alleyway. Without pausing or looking around, Cora stepped confidently out onto the grim streets of Urt ... and then promptly ran into someone.

'Oi! Watch it,' croaked the small man she had collided with.

Cora quickly righted herself. 'S-sorry.' But the small man was already moving away.

Cora shook herself. *Focus.* She took another deep breath, straightened her pack on her shoulders and set off down the street, careful not to run into any more small men.

She did her best to step in time with the crowd that headed towards the factory. Around her, the main street in Urt was filled with people. They pushed and grumbled, sniffed and mumbled as they journeyed to where they needed to go. Some were factory workers, dressed in stained and grimy overalls. Others were dock workers. A few were shop owners. There weren't any children. But Cora expected that. They would all be in school.

She felt herself relax as swirling scents of smoke and sea surrounded her as she walked. Cora breathed them in. Looking up, the sky was grey but the sun peeked out slightly from behind the blanket of clouds. *Perhaps collecting without Dot is going to be okay,* she thought.

Soon the street became wider and Cora could see that a few traders had set up stalls on either side of the road. Traders came in and out of Urt often, hoping to pick up some sought-after items or sell some not-so-sought-after items before moving on to the bigger, wealthier cities. They stood near their colourful, shiny wares, calling out to the crowd and Cora as she passed by.

'The prettiest jewels!'

'The finest rugs!'

'The softest clothes!'

'The warmest hugs!'

Cora stopped. She gave a small wave to the man who traded hugs. His name was Wilfred.

'Cora!' he said, spotting her. 'Where's Dot today?'

Suddenly, someone roughly pushed past her, someone else grumbled about the importance of manners in a crowd and then another someone stepped on the back of her heel. Deftly, Cora sidestepped through the crowd towards the hunched-over man. She took out one of the hickory buns Dot had put aside for her and handed it to Wilfred. The man's eyes lit up and he gave her a big hug in return.

'Be careful of the Trappers. They're out and about today.'

Cora swallowed. *Trappers*. Trappers was the name given to the thieves in Urt. They took what they wanted from whoever they wanted. And they didn't just take *things*. They took *people*, too. Trappers were dangerous and needed to be avoided at all cost. And what was worse was that Cora had completely forgotten about them. Hastily, she checked her pack to see if anything was missing. But nothing had been taken. She let out a sigh, thanked Wilfred and continued down the road, keeping her eye out for any sign of a Trapper.

'Have a beautiful day in beautiful Urt!' Wilfred called to her over the crowd.

Cora smiled. Nobody loved Urt more than Wilfred. Urt wasn't a place many people wanted to be. Not even the man the city was named after, Edwaldo Urt, wanted anything to do with it. She imagined him at parties pretending as though he was hard of hearing whenever the city was mentioned, 'Burt, you say? Never heard of it!'

Dot had told her that when an earthquake struck the city, a lot of people left and never came back, including Edwaldo Urt. Large parts of Urt were abandoned and forgotten in rubble. She tried to picture Urt when it was the beautiful, prosperous city Dot sometimes told her about. She looked up at the lopsided, grey and crumbling buildings next to her and tried to picture them new and sparkling instead of cracked and worn. She tried to picture the people beside her as cheerful and happy instead of grim and gruff.

Cora had small memories of being in another place once, before Dot had found her, but they were fleeting and unclear. A memory of pointed, red leather shoes in tall grass. Gazing into a bright sun, cool air on her skin. A yellow sundress and a soft laugh.

For Cora, Urt was what she had become used to. Just like her missing eye. She ran a hand over the red, bumpy scar that sat in its place. It was dark, unhelpful a lot of the time and to others it might've seemed ugly … but it just needed a little getting used to.

Dot had taught her that.

Cora looked over the top of the crowd and read the street signs to her left. *Horn. Fink. Lox.*

Turning down Lox, she soon left the shadows of the tall buildings and eventually came upon a row of empty houses. It was the first of the outer boroughs. She was where she wanted to be.

Hesitantly, Cora walked down the cracked garden path of the first dark house.

Chapter Three

The house was small but mostly still together. Cora could see that scavengers had taken some of the tiles from the roof and some of the glass from the windows. She walked up to the oak door and pushed it open. Stepping inside, the house smelt of dust and dampness. Rays of light shone down from above where the roof was missing its tiles.

Cora checked the drawers in the cabinets nearby first. They were empty. She moved to the kitchen and checked the cupboards. There was a small blue button sitting alone in one of them. She put it in her pocket.

Cora was quick just as Dot had taught her to be. But there wasn't much left to find in the house and no sign of Toe Tippins Shoe Polish, so she headed towards the front door. She stepped over a fallen, cracked roof tile and noticed something beneath it glisten in the light. Cora pushed aside the tile with her boot. Lying beneath it was a broken picture frame, and inside it a photograph of a family, smiling up at her. She bent down and picked it up. Carefully, she wiped the dust from it with her hand. Then Cora walked over to the fireplace and placed the picture frame on top of the mantle above it. *There*, she thought. *Better.*

She left the first house and moved on to the next. There wasn't much in the second house besides some twine, which Cora pocketed. And the third house had half a bar of soap, which Cora also pocketed.

The fourth and final house was two storeys high. It had a large garden and many rooms. Cora searched them all. When she found nothing, she walked out through a side door and into the backyard. She put her hands on her hips and looked around. The grass at her feet was brown and dry. She thought about where to go next. A button, some twine and half a bar of soap was definitely not enough to go back home with. And there was still no sign of the shoe polish. Then, looking up at the house, Cora noticed a small, round window sitting above the others.

That's weird. She had been through all the rooms in the house and couldn't remember seeing the small, round window in any of them.

Trust your instincts, she heard Dot's voice in her ear.

Nodding, Cora went back inside the house and took the stairs two at a time. She searched all the rooms once again. In and out, in and out. And just as she'd thought, there was no small, round window in any of them. That could only mean one thing.

'An attic,' she whispered in delight.

Cora looked upwards and searched the ceiling. And then, on the landing of the second floor, she found a tiny, broken latch poking out.

'Bingo,' she said happily.

Cora jumped up high, reaching as far as her arm could go. But the tips of her fingers went nowhere near the latch. She jumped again and again. And then, after a few more tries, she stopped, out of breath.

I might need a ladder, she thought.

Cora looked around her. Then she remembered seeing an old bookcase in one of the rooms. She found it and pushed it across the floor with both hands, as it creaked and groaned.

When it was positioned right underneath the latch, Cora stepped up carefully, until she could reach the tiny, broken latch on the ceiling. She pulled it and the door in the ceiling opened. She coughed and spluttered as dust fell onto her. Then she climbed the rest of the shelves and pulled herself up and into the hidden attic.

'Yes!' Cora cheered quietly. She held her hands up in the air at clapping from an invisible crowd. Then she took a bow.

Inside the attic stood a few pieces of old furniture: a desk, a lamp and a table. She checked the desk drawers but they were empty. She checked the lamp for a bulb but it was missing — as was the bulb from the ceiling light above. A little wooden clock sat on the table. Cora recognised it as being a cuckoo clock. She had seen one in one of Dot's books.

Gently, she moved one of the hands on the face of the clock. Then the clock suddenly sprang to life! Cora jumped in shock as music filled the attic and a little bird popped out of a pair of doors.

'Cuckoo!' it chirped. 'Cuckoo!'

Cora grabbed the wooden clock and pushed the bird back inside. The music stopped.

Be quick and be silent, Dot had said. Cora flinched at her words. She paused. She listened and waited, still holding the wooden cuckoo clock in a pair of now shaking hands. When there was only silence, Cora placed the clock back on the table as carefully as she could.

Scattered beneath the table were a few cardboard boxes. Cora rifled through the first one. In it was a collection of old crumpled-up newspapers.

'*The Urt Chronicle*,' Cora read as she flicked through the newspapers. Each of them was older than she was. And in the top right-hand corner of each was a picture of a man with an elaborately curled moustache. *Edwaldo Urt*. Cora was about to put the newspapers back in the box when she spotted something sitting at the bottom. It was a tiny, circular tin.

Cora's eyes widened. Her heart leapt. Picking it up, she turned it over and saw the words she had hoped were stamped across the front in fine, gold, cursive script.

'Toe Tippins Shoe Polish,' she breathed.

Cora ran her hand over the letters. She had done it! She had actually done it! Cora couldn't wait to race back home and show Dot. Standing up, she pushed the box back under the table and held on tightly to the shoe-polish tin in her hands. Maybe they could take it to the Mill Town trader together.

'Well, isn't this a surprise,' came a voice from behind her.

Chapter Four

Cora froze in place. All the joy she had felt from finding the shoe polish drained from her like water down a sink. She could have kicked herself. *The cuckoo clock*. Someone must have heard it. Swiftly, Cora pushed the shoe-polish tin up her coat sleeve and turned around.

Standing near the attic door was a short man and two teenage boys. *Scavengers*. Cora could tell straight away from their clothes. They were torn, dirty and either too big or too small for them. The short man had long, straggly hair and wore an old orange vest covered in buttons. He grinned at Cora and she noticed that a few of his teeth were black. The teenage boy next to him was round and had no hair at all. He wore a jacket that looked like it belonged to a man three times his size. The other boy had dark hair that fell over the left side of his face. His dark eyes peeked out at her in a cold stare.

'What have you got there, pretty?' asked the man in the orange vest.

Cora smiled her best smile. 'Just a box of old newspapers,' she said, kicking it to the side. She felt her voice shake as she spoke. *Stay calm*, she told herself.

'You're outnumbered, pretty,' said the man. 'Just hand over what you've found.'

'I haven't found anything,' she said. She did her best to try to sound believable.

The man took a step forward towards her. 'Then, *what* is that?' he asked, pointing at the cuckoo clock on the table.

There was a silence as all four of them looked over at the small, intricate timepiece.

'It looks like a clock, Eggs,' said the bald boy. 'To tell the time.'

The man shot him an agitated look. 'I know what a clock looks like, Knuckle!'

'Then why did you say —' the boy continued confused.

'Oh, never mind!' the man grumbled. 'Go and get it!'

Cora watched as the bald teenager walked over to the cuckoo clock. He held it up and looked at it. Then he did as Cora had done and pushed one of the hands on the clock face. Music filled the attic once more and the bird popped out of the doors.

'That should fetch a nice price,' the man said. 'Take it.'

The bald boy threw the cuckoo clock carelessly into the bag on his back.

'But I …' Cora tried before stopping helplessly as she watched the cuckoo clock disappear from sight. She felt a small pang of sadness. She had hoped to take the clock back home to Dot. The man was right. It would definitely fetch a nice price. Maybe even enough for a whole month's worth of oats. And the boy had just *thrown* it recklessly into his bag. Cora pressed her lips together but said nothing.

'How did you know this was up here, pretty?' asked the man. He squinted at her.

Cora shrugged. The less she said the better.

'You two cleaned this place out months ago, didn't you, Stink?' the man asked.

The boy with dark hair nodded. His eyes were on Cora. She tried to pay him no mind. Some people couldn't help but stare. It just needed a little getting used to, she felt like telling him.

'So a little girl found something you two couldn't.'

The teenagers straightened.

'And not only that,' the man continued, 'a little girl with *one* eye.'

'But —' the bald boy began.

'How were —' the one with long hair tried.

'Quiet!' the man yelled.

The teenagers glared at Cora.

'Look in the boxes, Knuckle,' the man barked, pointing to them at her feet. 'And this time try to use both your eyes.'

Cora took a step back.

The bald boy crouched down and pulled out the newspapers from the first box roughly. Then he searched the other boxes but only found the same.

The man's eyes rested on her once more. 'What else have you found?' he asked.

'Nothing else,' Cora said.

'Are you sure?' the man pressed.

Cora nodded.

'You wouldn't lie to me, pretty?' he asked, taking a few more steps towards her. Cora could see that in the man's belt three sharp knives glinted. Then out of the corner of her eye, she noticed that the boy with the long dark hair had also moved closer towards her. The bald boy did the same. She was being cornered.

Cora thought of Dot. What would she do? She took a step backwards. Then, with a heartbreaking *clank*,

the Toe
Tippins Shoe
Polish fell from her
sleeve and bounced
onto the attic floor.

No.

Time seemed to
slow as Cora watched
the precious tin skate
out of reach along the
attic floor and stop at
the scavengers' feet.

The three of them
looked curiously down at
the tin on the ground before the man in the orange vest
bent and picked it up. He turned it over and smiled a
black-toothed smile. Then he put the shoe-polish tin
swiftly in his vest pocket. 'Thank you, pretty.'

No, no, no.

'Please,' Cora croaked. 'Not that.' She tried to think quickly. What could she offer them? Then she remembered. 'Take these instead.' Hurriedly, Cora pulled out what was in her pockets. The half a bar of soap, the button and the twine she had found. 'For the shoe polish.'

Cora stood there with her items in her outstretched hands. It wasn't much but it might be enough. She hoped it was enough.

The man peered at her offering, before swiping the items from her palms and pocketing them. He smirked and then all three scavengers turned and headed for the attic door.

'Hey, where are you going?' Cora asked.

'Mill Town,' said the man. 'Shoe polish is in high demand.'

'Wait,' Cora said.

'Rule one of scavenging, pretty: never trust another scavenger,' said the man over his shoulder. The teenage boys laughed.

Cora felt sick in her stomach. She had just been tricked. Duped. Hoodwinked.

By the time she realised what had happened, the teenagers had already descended the bookcase. She ran across the attic towards the man in the orange vest, who had two feet on the bookcase.

'You can't,' she said, desperately grabbing onto his hand. 'Please.'

The man paused and opened his vests, showing her the knives on his belt. 'You don't want to do that, pretty,' he said warningly.

Cora let go of the man's hand, defeated. She couldn't do anything but watch as the last scavenger descended the bookcase, pushed it to the floor and then laughed as the three of them disappeared from view with not just her shoe polish and her cuckoo clock but also her half a bar of soap, her button and her twine.

Crud. Dot is going to be so mad.

Chapter Five

Cora dragged her feet as she walked. Her ankle was sore from having jumped down from the attic. She sighed. She had the shoe polish. She had it right in her hands! And she just ... let it get away. What was she going to say to Dot? That she had found the Toe Tippins Shoe Polish but then three mean scavengers took it from her after it had somehow fallen from where she had it hidden up her sleeve? And then she tried to trade it for the other things she had found but they took them too? She replayed the moment over in her mind. One minute the shoe polish was safely up her sleeve and the next minute it wasn't.

'Eugh!' Cora groaned. She kicked a stone on the road with her foot and watched it scuttle down the pavement as she walked over to the next house.

She stared up at it, squaring her shoulders. Cora remembered how Dot's eyes had glistened with confidence in her. She wasn't going to give up. She would find the shoe polish. Even if she had to look in every single house in the outer boroughs.

As Cora entered the next house, she made extra sure she was quick and quiet, and reminded herself not to touch anything she didn't need to. Especially clocks.

This house was an old house, the kind that creaked on its own. She searched it, room by room, paying extra attention to where she stepped. It didn't take long to find that the house was completely empty. She was in and out of there in minutes. Dot would have been impressed.

Soon, minutes turned into hours and the next house in the street turned into the seventh, and still there was no sign of Toe Tippins Shoe Polish.

When the seventh house came up empty, Cora sat down on the two back steps. It was well past lunchtime. She pulled out the last hickory bun from her pack. As she ate it, she briefly imagined herself searching for the scavengers who had taken the shoe polish from her, outsmarting them and then taking it back. She would say something clever such as, 'Looks like having one eye isn't so bad' or 'You've messed with the wrong girl' or 'What kind of name is Eggs anyway?' before vanishing into the night. But she wouldn't know where to even begin to track them down. And she wouldn't know how to outsmart them. And Dot would definitely not approve. And one of them had knives.

As the day went on, Cora continued to search the outer boroughs. House after house, room after room. When she reached the last house in the last borough, she began to think that the scavengers must have taken the only shoe polish left in Urt. Either that, or the people who lived in the outer boroughs never wore shoes.

Cora entered the last house in the street. It looked different from all the rest. The door and windows were round instead of square and the front garden still had tufts of green grass scattered by the path.

As she entered the house, there was an odd smell. It didn't smell bad. In fact, it smelt rather nice. Like something yummy was in the oven. But, looking around, the house was just as empty and falling apart as the previous houses she had searched.

Cora walked through the living room. On the floor sat a broken mirror. She looked down at it. Her quizzical reflection stared back. Then a green glimmer darted across the mirror's surface. Cora stopped and rubbed her eye. When the glimmer didn't return, she stepped over the mirror and into the kitchen.

She checked all the drawers and they turned up empty. The pantry that sat nearby was almost as tall as the ceiling. She craned her neck upwards, checking the shelves as best she could. But the top two shelves were too high up. She climbed the shelves of the pantry. When she reached the third shelf, the pantry shelves groaned with her weight. Cora reached up to the top shelf and ran her hand along it. She felt nothing but dust and dirt and cobwebs. And then, she felt something else. She grabbed hold of it with her hand and pulled it out. Cora looked at the dusty old shoebox she held in her hand.

What is a shoebox doing hidden inside a pantry? she wondered.

Excitedly, Cora jumped down from the pantry shelf. She lifted the lid off the shoebox and sitting inside it was … a pair of pointed, red leather shoes. Cora stared at them. They looked just like the ones from her memory. And there, sitting in the corner of the shoebox … was a tin of Toe Tippins Shoe Polish.

Cora bounced up and down on the spot happily. Then she closed the shoebox and placed it carefully in her pack. This time, she wasn't taking any chances. She needed to get home fast. No dawdling, as Dot would say.

As she walked back through the living room, her boot kicked something on the ground. It scuttled across the floor.

Cora stopped. *What was that?*

Curious, Cora walked over and sitting upturned on the floor was a small, square, wooden box.

She bent down and picked it up. It was made from a dark-coloured wood that was almost black, and the box itself was smaller than her palm. She had never seen anything like it.

'What are you?' she asked, looking it over with her eye. On one side of the box she found a white symbol burnt into the wood. She ran her finger over it. Then, as if she had pushed a button, one of the sides of the box popped open! Cora turned it over and looked inside but she couldn't see anything. Tentatively, she put her finger inside the box, grabbed and pulled something out. It was a piece of paper, rolled up in a tight scroll.

Carefully, Cora opened it. Written across the scroll in a neat font were words. At least, she thought they were words. They were looped and dotted in a way she couldn't understand. She tried to pronounce them.

'*Hegr howr ith,*' she said. '*Hegwer how er ith?*'

It was definitely another language. Maybe Dot would know how to read it? She placed the scroll back inside the box and closed it tight. Then she put the box in her pocket. At least she could go home with something more than the shoes and shoe polish ... even if she didn't know what it was.

Chapter Six

When Cora left the house, she saw that the sun had already begun to set. She didn't want to be finding her way home in the city at night. She walked fast, taking the main road back to the wall. Cora was so happy that she had found the shoe polish that she could have run all the way home. She could have skipped. But there were a few people around and she didn't want to draw attention to herself.

Cora turned down a street to her right. As she turned the corner, she stopped. Two people walked her way down the road. And they weren't just any two people. Cora saw with alarm that they wore long black cloaks. *Trappers*. Panic filled her up. *The shoe polish*. If they saw her, they would surely take everything she had. And who knows what else? This wasn't like coming across a group of scavengers. This was worse. Much worse.

Cora walked backwards slowly until she was behind the street corner once more. She looked around. She had to hide and fast. It wouldn't be long until the Trappers turned the corner, too. Nearby was a pile of rubbish. It was not big enough to hide in. Next to the rubbish was a grate that led to the sewers. It would have to do. She pulled the grate up and stepped inside, closing it above her. She looked around the tunnel. It was dark and cramped, and she was stepping in something wet and it stank. It stank worse than the time she and Dot had found Scratch's hidden collection of dead mice.

Above her, the Trappers turned the corner. Cora waited but they didn't keep walking. They stopped right near the grate.

Crud.

Both of them spoke in hushed whispers. Cora could only make out the odd word like 'shipment' and 'careful' and 'red'.

She had worked out that 'red' must have been one of the Trappers' names when she heard a hissing sound below her. Cora looked down. A fat rat crawled over her boot! She stifled a gasp and tried to shake it off but her other foot slipped in the water with a slosh. She lost her balance. Quickly, she put a hand on the side of the tunnel, saving herself from falling.

The Trappers stopped their whispers. Heart racing, Cora put a hand over her mouth and stayed very still. Had they heard her? She waited.

Then, thankfully, the Trappers walked away.

Phew. That was close.

Cora glared at the rat as it waddled unbothered down the tunnel. She remembered what Dot had taught her if ever she needed to hide from Trappers: always make sure they have gone. She stayed where she was for a few minutes longer just to be safe.

When Cora crawled out of the grate, the sun had almost completely set. She hurried, this time peeking around the corners of the streets before walking down them. She wasn't far from home. That is, if she didn't run into any more Trappers.

Cora turned down the main street in Urt. Unlike this morning it was now almost empty. The traders had packed up and gone. The factory and dockyard were closed. She couldn't wait to show Dot the shoe polish. She pictured her face lighting up. She pictured all the things the shoe polish would buy. Maybe she could get some new boots or a toy for Scratch.

As she walked towards the wall, she heard something familiar. It was soft at first but as she got closer to home her heart stopped. It was something she had heard many times before. The lullaby. Only this time it wasn't a drill.

Trouble.

Run.

Chapter Seven

Cora ran. But not away from the lullaby. She ran towards it. It was exactly what Dot had told her not to do. But she didn't care. She ran as fast as she could down the main street of Urt. Heart racing, her feet barely touched the ground. Her thoughts on only one thing. *Dot*.

She skidded to a stop when she reached the wall. Or, what used to be the wall. In its place, Cora gazed up at an enormous hole. She could see inside their home from where she stood on the street. Their things spilled out onto the ground.

Cora felt like she couldn't breathe. It was as though something had smashed right through the wall. Something huge.

'Dot!' she cried out in alarm. 'Dot!'

But only the sweet sound of the lullaby drifted out.

Cora scrambled into their home. She stumbled over

the mess on the floor and looked around. Everything was destroyed. Furniture had been smashed. Pots, pans, paper and food lay everywhere. Debris and rubble of floors and roofs covered the ground. The bookcase full of heavy, bound books lay in half.

A fear rattled her to her bones.

'Dot!' she screamed into the house.

But there was no answer. Just the lullaby.

She felt tears sting her eye.

'Scratch!' she cried.

Her vision blurry, she headed for the stairs. She stopped when she saw that most of them had been crushed beyond repair. Looking up, she could see that there was barely anything left of the upstairs. Her room. Dot's room. It was all gone. It was all in pieces at her feet.

'Dot!' she screamed once more.

She stood in the middle of their home, lost. Her mind whirled. It spun her in circles.

Think, Cora. Think!

But she couldn't. She could only see Dot's face. She held onto it. As she swiped the tears from her eye, she spotted something shiny by her feet. She picked it up. It was Dot's pocket watch. She ran her hand over it. Dot had told her about the day she had found it so many times. Cora pushed the story from her mind with a shake of her head and shoved the watch into her pocket. When she found Dot, she was going to give it back to her and hear the story again.

Cora began heaving and throwing books and furniture aside. Desperately, she searched through the rubble for any sign of Dot or Scratch.

'Dot!' she called out. 'Scratch!'

But again, there was no answer.

She pushed aside torn-apart books, lights, chairs. Cora knew that it wouldn't be long until scavengers would be all over the place. Taking what they could of their things. She had to protect them. For Dot.

Suddenly, the whole room shuddered. Everything shook around her. Cora tried to grab on to something, anything, as the floor and the roof trembled.

Then, from behind her, she heard a loud *POP*! Followed by another loud *POP*!

Cora spun around, a book in hand. Ready for whatever was waiting for her. For whatever had done this. But what she saw, she didn't expect to see at all.

Standing in the middle of her home, amongst the rubble and mess, were two plump and hairy men about half her size … with wings.

Cora blinked. Was she seeing correctly? She wiped the tears from her eye again.

'Miss, you're in terrible pudding,' said one of them. He had a small tuft of hair running down the middle of his head.

Cora stared at him, confused. *Pudding?* She shook her head. Her mind was more out of sorts than she realised.

'I mean, um, danger,' he said. 'You're in terrible danger.'

'What? Who are you?' asked Cora angrily. She brandished the book in her hand. 'And where did you come from?'

The two men looked at each other.

'Well,' said the other man who had hair coming out of his ears. 'We're fairies, of course.'

'Fairies!' Cora echoed disbelievingly.

Under her gaze, both of the fairies twirled on the spot, their wings flittering behind them.

To Cora, they certainly didn't look anything like fairies. At least, they were certainly nothing like the ones in Dot's books. The men in front of her weren't tiny or beautiful; they were plump and their teeth were crooked. They had not much hair on their heads and a lot of hair on their backs. And their clothes didn't fit them properly. Cora could see their hairy bellies poking out from beneath their shirts.

'Fairies?' Cora echoed again.

'I'm Tock,' said the man with the tuft of hair down the middle of his head. He gave a small bow.

'And I'm Tick,' said the one with hair coming out of his ears.

Tock looked over his shoulder worriedly. 'Now, please, miss. We have to go.'

Go? What are they talking about? Cora saw that the both of them kept looking over their shoulders at the hole in the wall. Like they were scared of something. But Cora didn't care. She couldn't care. She needed to find Dot and Scratch. Fairies or no fairies.

She looked at them. 'I'm not going anywhere. This is my home.'

'Was,' piped up the fairy called Tock. The other one elbowed him swiftly in the ribs.

Cora glared at them both. Then she turned her back on them and continued searching through the rubble. She needed to find Dot.

'Please, miss,' said one of the fairies. 'We're trying to help.'

'I have to find her,' said Cora. 'Dot!' she cried out. She tried with all her might to lift up the large bookshelf that lay in half on the ground. The bookshelf groaned as she lifted it up.

The fairies looked at each other.

There was nothing but books underneath it. She let it drop to the ground. 'She was here. She had to have been,' Cora said, more to herself than anyone else. Dot had made sure to warn her by playing the lullaby. *But warn her of what?*

Then the whole room shuddered. Everything shook around her. The floor and the roof trembled again. Cora looked up. The vibrations stopped. Then the ground shuddered once more.

'Uh-oh,' said Tock.

'Uh-oh,' said Tick.

Chapter Eight

The shaking and trembling became louder and louder. The rubble and debris bounced up and down at her feet. Cracks appeared in the walls that were still standing. *Was this another earthquake?* Cora wondered. Then chunks of ceiling started to crumble and fall on top of her. She shielded her head and looked up. The roof was going to collapse!

But Dot. And Scratch. Cora didn't want to leave. She couldn't. It was her home. The only one she had. And if she did leave, how would Dot and Scratch be able to find her? Their meeting place was on top of the wall. But now there was no wall.

She looked over at the fairies. But they weren't looking up at the roof. They weren't worried about the cracks in the wall. They weren't even facing her anymore. Instead, they flittered above the rubble and stared out into the street through the hole in the wall.

Cora's bracelet tingled at her wrist. She looked out through the hole too. And then she saw what the fairies saw. The shaking wasn't an earthquake at all.

Lumbering up the main street of Urt was a huge creature. Dark as the night, it was the size of a house. And with every bounding step it took, the walls around her shook. The creature shimmered like it was made out of shadows. Its yellow eyes looked like burning rings in the night.

And it was heading straight for them.

Cora wanted to run but she couldn't move. Her eyes were glued to the creature. She tried to lift her legs, she tried to speak, she tried to blink but it was as though something had a hold of her. As if … something was stopping her.

'Time to go,' said Tock, turning around.

Both of the fairies flew towards her. Then one of them touched her on the shoulder. There was a loud *POP!* and before Cora knew what was happening, the dark creature and her home disappeared from sight.

When Cora blinked, she found herself standing in the middle of a house.

She let out a breath she didn't know she'd been holding. She felt like she could talk again. She felt like she could move again.

'What *was* that?!' she gasped, the creature's yellow eyes still in her mind. She lifted her legs and her arms to make sure they were still working. Looking around, she recognised the room. They were inside the house she had been to earlier that day in the outer boroughs. The one where she had found the shoe polish in the shoebox.

'Why did you bring me here?' Cora asked.

'This house is protected,' said Tock.

'Can't you tell by the drapes?' asked Tick, pointing to the worn and dusty blue drapes hanging limply at the window.

Cora peered at them. They looked quite ordinary to her. Then, with a click of the fairy's fingers, the drapes pulled themselves closed with a snap!

'The drapes have a protection charm on them,' explained Tock.

Cora wasn't sure what the tattered pieces of cloth were going to do against that … creature.

In front of her, the fairies were pacing as they whispered to each other. They weren't very good at it because Cora heard every word.

'She has a witch's mark,' said one.

'Perhaps it wasn't us,' said the other.

'Hello?' Cora said. 'Was I the only one who saw that … that *thing*?'

Tick and Tock stopped pacing. They turned to her. Their faces still grim.

'That *thing* was a Jinx,' said Tock.

'A what?' asked Cora.

'A Jinx,' said Tick. 'Did you summon it?'

'What? Me? No,' said Cora.

The fairies stared at her, unbelieving.

Cora stared at them right back. 'I don't summon things. I can't. I don't know how. I'm a collector. *We* collect things,' she stopped as she thought of Dot once more. 'Wait. How did we get here? I have to go back.' Cora walked towards the door. The fairies flittered in front of her, blocking her path.

'You don't understand, I need to find Dot and my cat,' she said, trying to skirt past them. 'They could be hurt.'

'The Jinx knows your scent so it's of great igloo that you leave this city,' said Tick.

'Igloo?' echoed Cora, confused.

'Importance,' said Tock.

'It's of great *importance* that you leave this city,' said Tick. 'It won't be long until the Jinx finds your scent again.'

'My scent?' Cora responded, disgusted. She went to sidestep the fairy but he was too quick.

'When a Jinx knows your scent, it never forgets it,' said Tock.

'Can we give it something else to smell?' Cora tried. 'There are a few people in this city who smell pretty bad.'

Tick and Tock shook their heads.

She stopped trying to get past them. Instead she stood still and folded her arms. 'I don't know anything about magic or Jinxes or fairies. You have the *wrong* girl. Now please, let me pass.'

The fairies looked at each other.

'You know nothing about magic?' asked Tock.

Cora shook her head.

'But … you have a witch's mark,' said Tick.

'A what?'

Tick pointed to his left eye.

Cora paused. Then she shook her head. 'Th-that's a scar. I've had it since I was little. It just takes a little getting used to.'

Both of the fairies looked worried. Was it her scar? Why were they worried about that? It didn't mean anything.

Tock looked at Tick.

'Maybe it appeared on its own?' Tick suggested.

'When you saw the Jinx, could you move?' Tock asked.

Cora looked away. She hadn't been able to move a muscle. It had felt like she was frozen in place.

'W-what does it want?' Cora asked nervously. She wasn't sure she wanted to know the answer but the words had already tumbled out of her mouth before she could stop them.

Tick and Tock looked at each other.

Now Cora was sure she didn't want to know the answer.

'It … sort of … kind of … maybe … might … want to … *eat* you,' said Tock slowly.

Chapter Nine

Cora stared at the fairies, wide-eyed. 'It wants to *eat* me?!'

Tick and Tock nodded apologetically.

She groaned. How was this happening? She closed her eyes and rubbed her temples. Maybe this was all just a dream and she needed to wake up?

'Wake up,' she said to herself. 'Wake up, wake up.'

'What is she doing?' Tock asked Tick. Tick shrugged.

'I need to go back and find Dot and my cat,' said Cora. 'And when I find them, everything will go back to normal.'

'If your Dot and your cat were there when the Jinx came …' Tock said.

'It is unlikely that they —' began Tick.

'Don't,' Cora whispered. She turned away from the fairies. She couldn't think about that now. Dot and Scratch had to have gotten out. And she was going to find them.

The fairies looked at her sympathetically.

'It won't be long until the Jinx finds your scent again,' said Tock.

'We have to leave the city,' said Tick.

'I'm not leaving,' said Cora. She sat down on the ground. She thought about the Jinx finding her again. About its burning, yellow eyes. A shiver went up her spine. Stubbornly, she put her hands in her pockets. Then her hand hit something. Cora pulled the strange wooden box out of her pocket. The one she was going to tell Dot about but never did.

'Wait —' Tock stopped. 'Where did you get that?' he asked, alarmed.

Cora looked up. The fairies were now inches from her face, their eyes on the box in her hand.

'I found it,' she said with a shrug. 'In this house.'

'Oh,' said Tick. 'So that's where I left it.'

Tock glared at Tick. 'I knew we left the gateway too early. You had one job.'

'To be fair, travelling through a gateway while holding onto an ancient spellbox AND eating a big sandwich is a very difficult job,' said Tick.

Tock continued to glare at Tick.

'At least the sandwich was dishonest,' said Tick.

'Delicious,' corrected Tock.

Tick then turned to Cora and asked her sheepishly, 'Did you by any chance happen to open the spellbox?'

Cora nodded.

'Did you read what was inside?'

Cora nodded. 'I–I tried to but I couldn't pronounce it. I think it was in another language.'

'The spell was a Jinx,' said Tock, realising. He turned and elbowed Tick in the ribs.

'At least we now know what spell was inside the box,' Tick said, rubbing his side.

'Father is going to be so mad,' said Tock, pacing back and forth in the air.

'Madder than that time we set his beard on fire?' asked Tick.

'A lot madder,' said Tock.

A sinking feeling crept into Cora's stomach. 'What is it?'

'We were supposed to deliver that box to a spellkeeper in Urt for safe-keeping but Tick obviously got distracted by a large sandwich,' said Tock.

'A *very delicious* large sandwich,' added Tick.

'We were retracing our steps, looking for the box when we saw the Jinx heading straight towards you,' said Tock. 'When we saw your mark, we thought you might have summoned it.'

Tock held his hand out for the box and Cora gave it to him. With a long finger, the fairy pushed the symbol on the box and it popped open. Tock turned it upside down but instead of the scroll with strange writing, only ash fell out. Cora watched, confused, as the cinders fell to the ground in front of her.

'But-but there was a note inside it,' said Cora standing up. 'Honest.'

'It would have turned to ash soon after you read out the spell,' said Tick.

'So you're saying,' she began, trying to understand, 'that what I read out was a spell. And that spell brought that creature here?'

'Not just any spell,' said Tick.

'A curse,' said Tock.

A curse? She was *cursed*?

'A bad curse,' said Tick.

'The worst,' said Tock.

Cora groaned.

'Imagine if all the other curses were combined, this curse would be worse than all of those combined curses.'

Cora's stomach twisted in knots. Why did she have to find that box? Why did she open it? Was she really the cause for all of this? Was what happened to Dot and Scratch really because of her? Did that thing *eat* them? She tried to shake her head to be free of the thought but it stayed with her.

'What am I going to do?' she asked herself.

Tick and Tock looked at each other.

'We will help you,' Tock said. 'It's our fault you found the box in the first place. Well, Tick's fault.'

Tick shrunk low. 'Sorry about that.'

'But if we want to get out of here alive, we have to leave now,' said Tock sternly. 'The charm on this house isn't strong enough against a Jinx.'

'But what about Dot and Scratch? I can't leave them,' said Cora, torn.

'If they are alive,' said Tock gently, 'then you cannot go to them.'

'What?' asked Cora. 'Why not?'

'You will only bring the Jinx,' said Tick.

Cora swallowed, her mind spinning with thoughts. If the fairies were right, if that creature was after her then anywhere she went, it would follow. She couldn't let that happen. If Dot and Scratch were still out there, she had to protect them. And the only way to do that was to get as far away from them as possible.

Cora looked over at the fairies. She had made up her mind. 'What's the best way out of Urt?'

Chapter Ten

'We don't have much time,' said Tock. He flew over to the nearest window in the house and looked out. Then he stopped flying and with a click of his fingers, the fairy was suddenly dressed in a smart grey jacket and black suit pants. He had a hat to match. Tick stopped flying too, snapped his fingers and was dressed just the same, but in the opposite colours.

Cora stared at them.

'We need something of yours,' said Tick, grabbing her attention back.

'What? Why?' asked Cora.

'For the Jinx,' said Tick. 'Hurry now.'

Cora took off her pack and looked inside it. She pulled out a scarf. Dot had made it for her and would always sneak it into her pack in case she got cold. She couldn't part with it. She pushed it aside and dug further down. She found a stray sock at the bottom. It was her spare. Something Dot had said would come

in handy in case the socks she wore got holes in them.
She handed the sock to Tick.

Tick threw it on the ground, revolted.

'Hey,' said Cora.

'Let's go,' Tick said.

Their wings hidden from view beneath their
clothes, the fairies walked out the
door. With a final glance at
her sock, Cora followed
them. She looked hesitantly
around the street and
walked quickly to
keep up.

'What if someone sees us?' she asked, stepping in time with them.

'If anybody asks,' said Tock, 'we're on our way to a business meeting.'

'A business meeting?' spluttered Cora. *In Urt?* If they ran into scavengers and told them they were on their way to a business meeting, they would definitely laugh them right out of the city. And she didn't even want to think about what would happen if they ran into Trappers.

'It's when people meet to discuss business,' explained Tick.

Cora felt like telling Tick and Tock that they needed a better disguise but the closer they got to the city, the less Cora thought about scavengers and Trappers and disguises, and the more she thought about the Jinx. Her stomach lurched at every corner they turned. Were they getting closer to the Jinx? Or Dot? Or Scratch? She kept her eye out for any sign of them.

It wasn't long until they had left the outer boroughs behind and were walking along a street Cora recognised. Would it be the last time she would see these streets? These buildings? She couldn't believe that she was really leaving Urt. It didn't seem real. None of it did. That she was on the run? On the run from a creature made of shadows and burning, yellow eyes? A creature that wanted to *eat* her? And that two fairies were helping her? Dot would never believe it.

Then Cora remembered how she got to the house in the outer boroughs in the first place. One minute she was in her home and the next minute she wasn't.

'Can't you just …?' Cora said as she snapped her fingers. 'And make us appear somewhere else? With your magic?'

The fairies shook their heads.

'That takes a lot of energy,' said Tock.

'And we need to save our energy in case the Jinx returns,' added Tick.

Cora's stomach twisted nervously again.

'So we need to leave the city the old-fashioned way,' said Tock.

'Which is?' asked Cora, glancing behind her.

The fairies came to a stop and Cora bumped into them. She straightened and looked around. There was a grate in the middle of the road. It was just like the one she had climbed into to escape the Trappers.

'Through the sewers?' she asked.

The fairies smiled, nodding.

'We're going to leave the city *through* the sewers,' said Cora. *Was that even possible?*

The fairies continued to smile, still nodding.

'Below every city is a world of magic and wonder,' said Tick, wiggling his fingers.

Tock and Tick bent down and lifted the grate. They held it up and looked at her, waiting for her to get in.

'The sewers?' she asked again, just to be sure. 'There's magic in the sewers?'

And again the fairies smiled, nodding.

'Magic is everywhere,' said Tock. 'Now quickly, get in the sewers.'

Cora made a move to step down into the grate but was stopped by Tick.

'Wait,' the fairy said, holding up a hand. 'Before we go through, there's one more thing.'

'What?' asked Cora.

'What is your name?'

She stopped. She remembered the night Dot had found her, cold and alone. Dot had asked her what her name was, over and over. But she couldn't remember. So Dot had given her a name. She said it was her favourite name in all the world and she hoped she'd like it. A pang of sadness hit her like a wave as she remembered. She had never told Dot that she did. She liked it very much.

'It's ... it's Cora. Cora Bell.'

Chapter Eleven

With a squelch, Cora plunked down into the sewers for the second time that day. The sewer was filled with even more water than before. It splashed up and over her boots with a mucky slosh.

Ew.

The fairies followed her inside and closed the grate above them. Then Tick and Tock snapped their fingers and their business clothes disappeared. Their wings fluttered out behind them and they hovered just above the muck and water. The muck and water Cora had no choice but to stand in. She wished she had wings.

'This way,' said Tock. He flew down the dark tunnel with Tick close behind him.

Cora splashed through the foul sludge after them.

'It doesn't look very magical,' she said. *Disgusting* was the word she would have used. It looked and felt and smelt very disgusting.

'Just wait and see,' said Tock.

The tunnel became darker and darker the further they moved inside the sewer system. Soon Cora had no choice but to rely on only the fluttering noise of the fairies' wings to guide her. The tunnel bent and turned this way and that. The gunk she trudged through clung to her boots like glue. She had to keep both her hands running along the sides of the tunnel for balance. Just as she had done when she had needed to get used to walking and running with one eye. Dot had helped her balance on all kinds of things. Chairs, tables, even the top of the wall in Urt.

'Where are we going?' Cora asked.

'We might know someone who can help you,' said Tock. 'Maybe.'

'But first we need to stop somewhere on the way,' said Tick.

'Stop where?' asked Cora.

'You'll see when we get to the gateway,' said Tick.

'The gateway?'

'Yes, many magic-users use it for travel,' said Tock.

'It is protected by a guardian,' added Tick.

'A guardian?' asked Cora.

Then suddenly the tunnel beneath her disappeared. The sewer had taken a turn, this time dropping down below her into a pool. She wasn't paying attention and as she stepped one foot out in front of the other, there was nowhere for it to go but air.

'Ahh!' she cried out as she flew headfirst down the tunnel like a slide. Her arms outstretched in front of her, she slid through the filth and down the tunnel with a wet *whoosh*! The slide saturated her clothes, her hair, her face until she finally came to a stop, covered from head to toe, drenched in thick and stinky sewer water. She swiped the slop from her face and looked up at the fairies from the ground.

'We're here,' Tock said cheerily. The fairies had flown down the drop easily.

'We should have tried that,' said Tick to Tock. 'It looked like fun. Was that fun?' he asked her.

Cora could only groan in response. She stood up, sopping wet and dripping, and wiped what sludge she could from herself. *Great.*

Ahead of them, Cora could see a small glow lighting up the end of the dark tunnel. The fairies flew towards it.

With a squelching shuffle, Cora followed after them. They stood waiting for her by the light. It came from a small lamp resting on the ground.

The fairies waited.

Cora waited too. She looked around questioningly. Was there something she was missing?

Then Tick said, 'Guardian, meet Dora.'

She was about to correct the fairy when a man stepped out of the shadows nearby.

Cora stepped back.

'Wilfred?!' she gasped.

Standing in front of her was the trader of free hugs, just as she had seen him that morning.

'Hello, Cora,' he said, with a smile.

'What are you doing here?' she asked.

'He is letting us through the gate,' said Tock as though it were obvious.

'Wait a minute … you're the guardian?!' she asked.

Wilfred nodded proudly.

Then he bent down and with what looked like a piece of chalk, drew a line over the ground of the sewer tunnel in the shape of a circle. The line then glowed a pulsating bright blue and the ground inside it disappeared, a swirl of blue light in its place.

'Follow us,' said Tock.

'And don't touch anything,' said Tick.

The fairies jumped into the swirling blue light, which swallowed them up. And then with a loud *POP!*, they were gone.

Cora looked from the swirling ground to Wilfred and then back again. *I'm supposed to jump into that?* She hesitated. Was she doing this? Was she really doing this? Leaving Urt? Leaving Dot? She looked over at the trader of free hugs, unsure.

'You might want to jump soon,' he said.

'Wilfred,' Cora said softly, 'Dot is missing. There was this ... creature, and I don't know what happened but she, and Scratch, they're ... I don't know where.'

'I'll look for her,' said Wilfred with a stern gaze. 'And your cat.'

Cora looked at him, a tear filling her eye. She nodded a thank you as she brushed the tear away.

'And Wilfred,' she added.

'Yes, Cora?'

'If you find Dot, tell her ... tell her I'll be back. I promise I will. And that ... and that ... I'm sorry.'

Wilfred nodded.

Then, taking a deep breath and closing her eye, Cora jumped into the swirling blue light below.

Chapter Twelve

It felt like she was falling. The blue light around her was so bright she could see it from beneath her eyelid. All around her was the sound of rushing water. Loud, rushing water. Cora put her hands to her ears.

Then, curious, she opened her eye and immediately regretted it. She didn't just *feel* like she was falling, she *was* falling. Instinctively, she reached out to save herself from hitting a ground that could appear at any moment but this made her swirl upside down.

'Ahh!' she cried out but she couldn't hear it. The blue light had snatched the sound of her voice away.

She spun as she fell. She kept spinning. And kept falling. Then, suddenly, the blue light around her started to get smaller and smaller.

Oh no?! Is it closing?

Cora panicked. What would happen if it closed while she was still falling? She tried to right herself, to gain her balance in the swirling blue light. Then a small, black hole appeared below her and she spun towards it. It got closer and closer. She closed her eye as it sped up towards her.

Please, please, please.

Then there was a loud sucking noise, a *POP!* and an *oof* as Cora landed on something.

'Ow,' she said, rubbing the back of her head.

'Finally,' came a fairy's voice from nearby.

'We thought the gateway would close without you,' said the other. 'That would have been bad.'

She opened her eye to find herself lying on her back, on top of a pile of rubbish bags. Tick and Tock looked down at her.

'Where am I?' she asked, sitting up.

'You are in the trash,' said Tock.

'I can see that,' she said, plucking and tossing aside a banana peel that was stuck to her hair. 'But in the trash where?'

'Mill Town,' said Tick.

Mill Town. Dot had said the trader who wanted the shoe polish was from Mill Town. Her head pounded. She put a hand to it. She felt queasy in her stomach.

'Travel sickness,' said Tock.

'You'll get used to it,' said Tick.

Slowly, Cora got out of the rubbish bags and

carefully stood up. She stumbled. It felt like she was still spinning and falling.

The sky was dark. Looking up, Cora could see that they were standing next to a large, white house in the middle of a field.

'Stay here,' Tock said to Cora. 'We'll be back.'

'Wait,' said Cora. She didn't want them to leave. She didn't want to be left alone in the dark somewhere in Mill Town while there was still a Jinx after her. 'You can't leave me here. What if the Jinx finds me?' And how did she know they weren't going to leave and never come back? 'Take me with you,' she said. 'Please.'

Tick and Tock looked at each other.

'We have to be as quick as possible,' said Tock softly. 'In and out.'

'But what if —' Tick began, looking at Cora.

'In and out,' repeated Tock.

Tick nodded.

'Follow us, stay close,' said Tock. 'And keep quiet.'

Then both of the fairies flew towards the side of the house.

Cora took one step and stopped. Her legs felt all wobbly. When she looked down to make sure they were still her legs, she realised that she was no longer covered in disgusting sewer water. She was dry and clean. That was something, at least. Slowly, she followed the direction the fairies flew in and when she reached them, she was glad to feel her travel sickness start to wear off.

Tick and Tock stood atop a pair of steps outside a small door on one side of the house. The door, Cora noticed, was fairy-sized. A gold plaque stood next to the entrance.

Drake Manor, Cora read.

Tock knocked once on the door, then twice and then once more.

The door swung open with a creak and Tick and Tock flew inside. Awkwardly, Cora bent down to fit through the door and then shuffled inside on her hands and knees.

She stood up on both feet when she got inside. In front of her was what looked like a small kitchen and standing nearby was a man dressed all in black. He wore a small set of glasses and a bored expression.

'He is in his study,' the man said to Tick and Tock.

The fairies nodded and flew out of the kitchen, motioning for Cora to follow. Cora smiled politely at the man. He raised an eyebrow at her in response. Then as Cora walked past him, she noticed something that made her eye go wide. Poking out of the back of the man's pants ... was a long, furry tail.

She stopped. Then Tick quickly grabbed her by
the hand, a finger to his lips and led her out of the
kitchen.

'Did he —' whispered Cora, when they were out
of earshot.

'This way,' Tock whispered back, cutting her off.

As they walked into the next room, three polished couches sat empty and large portraits lined the walls. Another man dressed all in black but without a tail, dusted one of the portraits with a feather duster. The portrait was of a woman and a child.

They entered the next room and it was exactly the same. Three polished couches and portraits on the walls. Cora had never been inside such a strange house. There was nothing like it in Urt. And it was oddly cold and dark. Perhaps it was leftover travel sickness but there was something about the house that Cora couldn't quite put her finger on. A feeling that crept over her.

Soon, they came to a dark hallway. The floor and the walls of the hallway were covered in emerald tiles. As the three of them walked down it, Cora could hear her boots clipping and clapping along the tiled floor, her steps echoing down the hallway. She tried to walk more quietly.

At the end of the hallway were large double doors. Tick and Tock looked at each other and then Tock repeated the knock from earlier. There was a pause. They waited.

'Enter,' came a deep voice from behind the door.

Chapter Thirteen

Tick pushed open the double doors and flew into the room. Cora followed close behind. She had expected more green tiles, more dark and dim lighting, perhaps another man with a tail, but unlike the hallway and the rest of the house, the room they had entered wasn't dimly lit or dark. There was a fireplace ahead of them and rows of books in tall bookcases that lined three out of the four walls. Cora looked around in awe. It was perhaps not only the biggest room she had ever seen but it was also most certainly the biggest collection of books she had ever seen. There were ten times the number of books that Dot had.

At least.

Standing with his back to them in front of the fireplace was a man. He wore a long cloak that came down to his knees and boots that came up to his knees.

'Deliver what you need to and get out,' said the man, his back still towards them. The light from the fire cast a stretched shadow of him across the floor and against one of the walls.

Mr Drake, Cora presumed.

Tick and Tock looked at each other, uncertain.

Cora realised that since they had arrived in Mill Town, Tick and Tock had been looking at each other the same way they looked at each other when they found her in Urt right before the Jinx showed up. Like they were frightened.

Who is this man?

'Mr Drake, sir … we were instructed not to leave until you open it,' said Tock.

The man muttered a curse that Cora couldn't quite catch. Then Mr Drake spun sharply around on one heel. His face looked like it was stretched across his bones. His dark hair was grey at the sides, long and untidy, and his mouth curved downwards into a grim line. He stared at Tick and Tock, annoyance in his eyes.

Tock held out a box in his hand. Mr Drake strode towards him and snatched it up. He pressed a finger to the side of the box and just like Cora's did, it opened. He pulled out a piece of paper from inside.

As she watched him read it, a glint caught Cora's eye. It was a black ring, wrapped around one of his fingers. It looked like obsidian stone. From what Dot had told her, obsidian stone was incredibly rare.

Mr Drake's eyes glanced away from what was written on the piece of paper. Then he scrunched it up and threw it over his shoulder, where it caught alight in the burning fireplace.

'You can tell Miss Daphne that the council won't abide by this and neither will I!' Mr Drake said angrily. 'She is to come home. At once!'

Then he threw the message box at Tick and Tock. The fairies shielded their faces with their hands as the box flew at them with surprising speed.

'Hey!' said Cora instinctively. The moment the word left her mouth, she knew it was a mistake, for the man's dark eyes found hers.

Crud.

Tock had told her to be quiet. Why couldn't she just be quiet?

The man's eyes shifted and settled on where her eye once was. She stood a little straighter under his gaze.

'And who is this?' Mr Drake asked Tick and Tock, his eyes still on her.

'Nobody,' said Tock a little too quickly.

'Nobody?' Mr Drake echoed doubtfully.

'Just a simple street urchin,' said Tick.

A street urchin? Cora couldn't help but feel offended.

'Why is a street urchin travelling with fairies?' Mr Drake asked. 'That seems ... peculiar.'

'She's helping us with our deliveries,' said Tock.

'Does she speak?' Mr Drake asked, stepping closer.

'Not really,' said Tock, moving in front of Mr Drake.

'She has a rare ... dishwasher,' said Tick, also moving in front of Mr Drake.

Mr Drake paused and raised an eyebrow at them.

'Disease,' corrected Tock. 'A rare disease that doesn't let her speak very much.'

With a scoff, Mr Drake pushed past the fairies and continued towards Cora.

Cora didn't know what to do. Should she run? Hide? Try to distract him? She saw the fairies out of the corner of her eye shake their head at her, eyes wide.

Mr Drake came to a stop when he was within an arm's length of her. His eyes, searching her face for something.

A cold feeling crept over her.

'In this world … that,' he said, pointing to where her eye used to be, 'can mean … many things.'

Cora swallowed. As she reached up to touch her face, her bracelet tingled on her wrist.

Mr Drake's gaze moved from her scar to her wrist.

'I thought I felt something,' he said. Mr Drake then reached out a hand towards her.

Suddenly, Cora couldn't move. It was like the Jinx had her again. But the only thing she could see was Mr Drake's glowing eyes. The green orbs bore into her like hooks. Then she *felt* them. They were searching for something. A feeling squirmed inside her and she pushed back against it. Then like a wall was put between them, she could move again.

Mr Drake took a step back, his eyes wide with shock.

'Look at the time,' said Tock, flying towards them and stopping to hover in between Cora and Mr Drake's hand. The fairy looked at his wrist where there wasn't a watch.

Tick flew in between them too, trying to block Cora from Mr Drake's view. 'We have so many more deliveries.'

'So little time,' said Tock.

'Can't stay to chat,' said Tick. 'Come along, street urchin.'

Mr Drake ignored them, his eyes still drilling holes into Cora's.

Then Tick and Tock turned, placed their hands on her shoulder and with a *POP!* the room and Mr Drake's piercing eyes disappeared from view.

Chapter Fourteen

When Cora opened her eye, she found herself in a dark room. She couldn't see anything at all. She rubbed her eye, just to make sure it was working properly.

'That was close,' said Tock, from somewhere nearby. It sounded like he was out of breath. Then there was a soft click and a small light bulb that dangled from the ceiling flicked on.

Cora looked around. It looked like they were in an old, unused cellar. Tick and Tock flew in front of her.

'Who was that man?' Cora asked. 'And why was he so … strange?' The cold, tingling feeling still crept over her like a spider.

'Archibald Drake,' said Tick.

'Is he a —' Cora began.

'Warlock?' finished Tock.

'Yes,' said Tick.

A warlock?! She was going to say a politician or a businessman but a ... 'A warlock?!' she echoed.

'We have to get her to The Hollow,' said Tick.

'The Hollow?' Cora asked.

'It's too late,' said Tick. 'Fizz will be by the gate.'

'Fizz?' Cora asked.

'We'll deal with him when we get there,' said Tock. 'We have only days until the Jinx finds her scent again.'

Cora watched the two fairies argue. A pounding began in her ears and then it moved to her head. She tried to shake it away but couldn't. Since leaving Drake Manor something in her was rattled. The words of the warlock repeated themselves over and over in her mind. *That can mean ... many things.* And the noise was getting too much. All of it was getting too much.

'Stop!' Cora cried out.

Tick and Tock stopped arguing and turned to her, surprised.

'Please,' began Cora, 'can we just ... stop?'

She sat cross-legged on the ground and put her head in her hands. What was she doing? She should have just stayed in Urt and looked for Dot and Scratch. Now she was somewhere else, maybe in Mill Town, she wasn't sure. The Jinx still wanted to eat her, she was still cursed and she had now come face to face with a warlock. Things were going from bad to worse.

'I wish Dot was here,' she said as she wiped a tear away from her eye. She thought about what Dot would do. She put a hand in her pocket and ran her fingers over Dot's pocket watch, her words echoing in Cora's mind, *You're stronger than you think.*

Tick and Tock paused. Then they flew down and sat cross-legged on the floor in front of her.

'We can't stop,' said Tick. 'Not yet.'

'There isn't time,' said Tock softly.

Cora groaned. She knew there wasn't time. A feeling of defeat washed over her.

'We're almost home,' said Tick.

'The gateway is just over there,' said Tock. Cora looked up. Tock pointed to a pile of dirty, squashed boxes that sat in the corner of the cellar.

Another gateway? Here? Cora hesitated. Then Cora saw that on the walls above the boxes was a collection of bright sparkling stones embedded into the bricks. They glistened different colours in the dark.

'You said the Jinx is only days away,' said Cora.

Tock looked at Tick.

'Curses can be broken,' said Tick.

'It has happened before,' said Tock.

'Really?' Cora asked.

'Maybe,' said Tick.

Cora studied the fairies. There was a confidence

in their eyes. Almost like the way Dot looked at her sometimes. She had to get rid of the curse if she was ever going to see Dot again. Cora found herself nodding.

Standing up, they walked over to the boxes in the corner. Tick and Tock pushed them to the side. On the wall, hidden behind the boxes, was a hole. The hole looked just big enough for them to squeeze through, one at a time.

Are there places like this hidden in every city? Cora wondered.

One by one, they went through the hole in the wall. The fairies flew through first and then Cora followed, crouched down low to fit.

When she got to the end, Tick and Tock were waiting for her in a small room with a ladder. They flew over to a man who was asleep on the ground. His loud snores echoed around them.

Another guardian? Cora thought.

Then Tock kicked the man's boot.

The man jumped, startled awake.

'Wah-ha!' he cried out in fright, looking around him. Then, glancing up, the man saw Tick and Tock hovering above him, their hands on their hips.

He sat up quickly. 'S-sorry! I must have d-dozed off!'

The man stood up and bowed apologetically to the fairies. Then he pulled out a piece of chalk, just like Wilfred had, bent down and drew a square on the ground. The line glowed a bright blue and then the ground fell away, a swirling blue light in its place.

Cora peered down at it nervously. This time she was not going to dawdle. She would jump at the same time as the fairies. She watched as Tick and Tock flew near the pulsating blue square. She stepped up next to them.

Then Tock held out a hand to her.

She grabbed it gratefully.

Taking a deep breath, she jumped with the fairies into the light.

Cora kept her eye open this time and watched as blue wrapped around her. The three of them floated in the light before being pulled downwards. The deafening sound of rushing water wasn't so bad the second time around. Then Tock let go of her hand and made a diving motion to her.

Cora nodded.

The fairies dove downwards like they were in a pool of water. Quickly, they flew away from her.

Cora straightened and then made a diving motion, too. She sped down towards the fairies. When she reached them, Tick turned to her and gave her a thumbs up.

Then, like before, a small, black hole appeared below them. It got closer and closer. She closed her eye as it sped up towards her. Then she noticed Tick and Tock lean backwards, falling feet first towards the hole. Cora did the same. Then there was a loud sucking noise, a *POP!* and an *oof* as Cora landed on something that was this time surprisingly soft.

Chapter Fifteen

It was Tock.

'Ow,' he said from beneath her.

Cora scrambled to her feet. 'Sorry! Sorry!'

The fairy lay on the ground, his face in the dirt.

'Are you hurt?' Cora asked worriedly. She bent down and looked him over. Had she just broken a fairy?

'My wings are crushed and I can't move my legs,' said Tock into the dirt.

'What?!' gasped Cora horrified. She *had* broken a fairy.

'Tock, stop playing,' said Tick, flying next to her.

With a laugh and a twirl, Tock flew upwards, clearly not broken. He stopped in mid-air, a big smile on his face.

Cora glared at the fairy but was relieved to see that he was perfectly fine. She looked around them. They had landed somewhere outside. Large oak trees dotted their surroundings and there was a small, open clearing that jutted out onto a cliff nearby. It was still night-time and strung up across some of the oak trees were tiny, twinkling lights. Cora could hear the gentle sound of music coming from somewhere close.

'Where are we?' she asked.

Tick and Tock flew over to the clearing and looked out over the edge of the cliff. Cora followed. Carefully, she peered over it too.

'Welcome to The Hollow,' said Tock.

Below them, nestled in a valley, was a village. Huts of all different shapes and sizes sat together. They had rounded, brightly coloured roofs and, just like in the oak trees, small lights were strung up along each of the huts, basking the valley in a pretty glow. To the side of the village, was a large lake. From up high, Cora could see the shapes of a few fairies walking and flying around the village. She thought it was beautiful.

'Is this your home?' Cora asked.

Tick nodded proudly.

'Who goes there?' came a small voice from behind them.

Tick and Tock groaned.

'Follow us,' whispered Tock.

'Stay close,' whispered Tick.

'And —' added Tock.

'Keep quiet,' finished Cora. 'I know.' She had well and truly learnt her lesson at Drake Manor.

Tick, Tock and Cora turned around to face the owner of the voice. Hovering behind them was a fairy. He looked similar to Tick and Tock but instead of having hair coming out of his ears or down the middle of his head, he had hair coming out of his nose. Cora noticed with slight unease that the fairy's nose hair went out of his nostrils, past his mouth, over his chin and down his chest where it was plaited into a knot that ended just above his belly, which, like Tick's and Tock's, also stuck out of his shirt. The fairy held what looked like a spear in one hand and a small, glowing orb floated in the air near him, lighting the space on the ground around him.

'Hello, Fizz,' said Tock.

'Tock,' said Fizz with a nod.

'Hello, Fizz,' said Tick.

'Tick,' said Fizz with a nod. The fairy's eyes then rested on Cora.

'Who is this?' Fizz asked, pointing the spear at her.

Cora stared back and said nothing.

'She has a message for King Clang,' said Tock.

'We need to see him immediately,' added Tick.

Fizz looked at Cora up and down. 'It's late,' he said with a shake of his head.

'We know,' said Tock.

'But it is urgent,' said Tick.

Fizz paused. He looked at the fairies distrustfully out of one eye.

'This better not be another one of your tricks,' said Fizz, pointing a finger at them.

'Tricks?' questioned Tick.

'Us?' added Tock innocently.

Cora allowed herself a small smile in the dark.

Then after a moment, Fizz gave a small and almost imperceptible nod to Tick and Tock. 'Follow,' he said. He turned in the air and made his way along the tree line, the glowing orb lighting his way.

Tick and Tock followed the fairy, with Cora close behind.

The tree line where Fizz led them sloped downwards and soon they began to descend the cliff. To their left, the twinkling lights looped through the trees in a sparkling trail, guiding them towards the village. When they got to the bottom, they walked along a small path that opened out onto the valley. A large arch made from branches, vines and flowers stood at the entrance to the village. The fairies fluttered through. Cora stared up as she walked beneath it. It was so big and so intricately woven. She wondered how many fairies had made it. She had never seen anything like it.

Inside the village, it was much the same. The huts were made out of neatly woven branches, vines and flowers. As they walked, fairies flittered by her. Some nodded to Tick and Tock, others nodded to Fizz. Cora noticed wind chimes hanging outside some of the huts. They tinkled softly in the night air.

Soon, Fizz came to a stop outside a large hut. Unlike the rounded ones that sat around the village, this one was bigger, its roof was pointed and it had a bright pink ribbon attached to a pole out the front of it. A small line of fairies stood outside the entrance.

'Wait here,' said Fizz, moving them to the front of the line. Then Fizz darted inside the hut.

'Don't forget to bow,' said Tock.

'Bow?' Cora questioned. There were murmurs from the line behind her. She looked back and locked eyes with a pale man who stood tall above the fairies. He had shaggy brown hair and held on tightly to a walking stick.

Then Fizz poked his head out of the king's hut.

The man with shaggy hair hobbled up to the fairy. 'Please, I need to see the king,' he pleaded.

Fizz shook his head and motioned for Cora, Tick and Tock to enter instead.

Tick and Tock flew into the hut. Cora followed behind them, whispering a small 'sorry' to the man with shaggy hair as she passed.

The hut was a large, round room. The floor was covered in red rugs and the roof was decorated with ribbons and flowers. Looking around, Cora spotted a long table nearby with plates and bowls of fruits and berries. At the end of the room was a stage and sitting in a large, comfortable chair with large comfortable cushions was a fairy twice the size of Tick and Tock, and twice as hairy.

Clang the Fairy King.

Chapter Sixteen

With a hand, King Clang motioned for the three of them to come closer. Tick and Tock flew over to the stage and then together, the fairies bowed before the king. Cora walked quickly over to stand next to the fairies. From where she stood, she noticed that the king's seat was far too big for him, his small feet dangled, nowhere near the ground.

The King's eyes rested on her questioningly.

Clumsily, Cora did a small curtsy. But should she have bowed?

'Fizz tells me it's urgent,' said the fairy king. His eyes looked at them sleepily from beneath two very hairy eyebrows. He straightened the small crown on his head and stifled a yawn. 'You know I like to be in bed at this time.'

'Yes, King Clang,' said Tock, nodding.

'And we're very sorry for the late hour,' said Tick.

'When we were in Urt —' began Tock.

'Burt?' asked King Clang, confused.

'No, Urt,' said Tick. 'Remember? You had asked us to make an urgent delivery to the spellkeeper?'

King Clang nodded, remembering. His small eyes moved from Tick and Tock to rest on Cora. He then glanced at where her eye used to be.

'Well, we accidentally might have lost the ancient spellbox —'

'You lost it?!' roared King Clang.

'And Dora —' said Tock, motioning to Cora.

'Cora,' corrected Tick.

'And Cora,' repeated Tock, 'found it.'

The king relaxed in his chair.

'But,' added Tick, 'she opened the box, read the spell … and now has the curse of the Jinx.'

The king's eyes widened. He straightened in his seat and pointed to Cora. His mouth opened and closed like a fish. '*She* is cursed? With the Jinx curse?' The fairy king was now very much awake.

Tick and Tock nodded.

'What were you thinking, bringing her here?!' King Clang bellowed at Tick and Tock. 'A cursed! In The Hollow!'

'Your Majesty —' tried Tick.

King Clang flew down from his seat. He came to a stop in the air when he was face to face with Tick and Tock. 'You not only lose the ancient spellbox I trusted you to deliver but you have also put your entire people in danger!'

Tick and Tock looked down.

'Please,' said Tick.

But the king shook his head, his small crown wobbling. 'She must leave! Immediately!' he spat, throwing a glare at Cora.

'It was my fault —' said Tick.

'I don't want to hear it!' roared King Clang.

Cora couldn't help herself. She stepped forward. 'Please, Your Majesty,' she said, 'they were just trying to help me.' King Clang's angry stare settled on her. Cora had a sudden urge to step back but instead, she stood tall, meeting the king's gaze.

'She was able to summon a Jinx,' said Tick.

'That means she's *something* powerful, right?' added Tock.

'Powerful?' Cora spluttered. '*Me?*' What were they talking about?

King Clang paused, looking at her. 'Are you a witch?'

'No,' said Cora. 'At least, I don't think I am.'

'Then how did you summon a Jinx?' asked the king.

'I … just read what was inside the box,' Cora said innocently.

The king's eyes squinted at her from beneath his big brows. He lifted a hand and stroked one of them in thought.

'How long?' King Clang asked Tick and Tock.

'Two days,' said Tick.

'Maybe three,' added Tock.

The king paused, thinking. 'I'll give you one,' he said. 'Then I want her gone.'

Tick and Tock nodded.

'Starting now,' said the king.

Tick and Tock hastily bowed.

'Now?' Cora asked.

Then Tick and Tock flew in front of her, ushering her towards the entrance. She took one last look at King Clang as she walked away from him. He looked back at her, his brows creased in worry, until she was out of the hut.

Outside, Tick and Tock veered to the left of the king's hut and flew through the village.

'Where are we going?' Cora asked as she followed. They turned down a small path between two huts that headed towards the lake. They were in a hurry. Cora had to jog to keep up.

'We're going to see if the godmothers can help you,' said Tock.

'The godmothers?' she asked.

'The fairy godmothers.'

Chapter Seventeen

Tick and Tock knocked on the door of a round hut. It wasn't as big as the king's but it was bigger than most of the other huts that sat around it. They waited. The lights were on inside.

'The godmothers are the oldest fairies in the kingdom,' said Tock.

'If anyone can help you, they can,' said Tick.

'Or maybe a witch,' added Tock.

Cora wasn't so sure about the fairies' plan. If they only had a few days until the Jinx found them, then shouldn't they be running? Shouldn't *she* be running? Shouldn't she be somewhere far, far away by now?

The door to the hut creaked open and a fairy with white hair and small glasses on her nose poked her head out.

'It's late,' she said.

'It's urgent,' said Tock.

The old fairy looked at Cora and where her eye used to be. The fairy tilted her head at her, intrigued. Then she opened the door wider for all three of them to enter.

Stepping inside the hut, Cora was greeted with a wall of warmth and the smell of something delicious. In the living room in front of her, there were chairs and furniture. A cabinet full of teapots sat to the side. Knitted blankets were draped over the chairs. Perhaps the fairies wouldn't mind if she took just a small nap.

Cora was about to ask when another fairy flew into the room. She wore a small nightcap atop her curly, white hair.

'Fairy godmothers,' said Tock. 'This is Cora.'

'She is —' began Tick.

'Cursed,' said the old fairy with the glasses.

'How did —' started Cora, surprised.

'We have seen many cursed in our time, dear,' said the old fairy with glasses. 'You all have that same look about you.'

'Look?' Cora resisted the urge to touch her face.

'Fear,' said the old fairy with the nightcap.

Cora swallowed. *Yep.*

'It will be alright,' said the fairy with the glasses. She took off Cora's pack and set it down. Then the fairy with the nightcap held out a hand for Cora's coat. She gave it to her.

'What kind of curse do you have, dear?' asked the fairy with glasses.

'A Jinx?' Cora replied hesitantly.

The fairy godmothers shared a look. Cora was afraid of that.

'Well, let's see what we can do,' said the fairy with the nightcap. 'Stand over there. Arms out.' She pointed to the middle of the room.

Cora walked over and held out her arms.

The fairy godmothers flew around her. They inspected her hair, her clothes, her shoes.

'Remember all the cursed ones, Squeak?' asked the fairy with the nightcap.

'There was Tabitha Ant,' said Squeak, the old fairy with the glasses. 'She was cursed by her sister.'

'And Millard Fort,' said the old fairy with the nightcap. 'He got on the wrong side of a warlock.'

'Oh, and Belton Trout,' said Squeak. 'He was a nice boy, wasn't he, Squash?'

'What happened to them all?' Cora asked. 'Did you break their curses?'

'Oh, no, dear. They're all dead,' said Squash.

Cora groaned. So far the fairy godmothers weren't helping at all.

Then Squeak stopped. She looked at Cora curiously through her spectacles. 'What are you, dear?' she asked.

'Who am I? I'm Cora,' she said, confused.

'No, *what* are you?' repeated the fairy. 'Not w*ho*.'

Cora didn't know how to respond.

'Can you talk to animals?' asked Squeak, resuming her circling.

Cora shook her head.

'Can you read minds?' asked Squash, lifting up her hair to look in her ear.

Cora shook her head.

'Can you raise the dead?' asked Tick.

Cora shook her head firmly.

'Can you play the flute really, really well?' asked Tock.

'What?' Cora asked.

Tock shrugged. 'Some say it's a gift.'

Cora definitely could not do any of the things the fairies mentioned. But what did all of it have to do with the Jinx? Dot's words echoed in her mind. *You're not like others, Cora.* She shook them away.

Then the fairies stopped flying around her. They fluttered in the air near her right arm, their eyes on the bracelet on her wrist.

'This bracelet,' began Squeak, tapping the white chain on her wrist, 'where did you get it?'

'I've had it ever since I can remember,' Cora said with a shrug.

The fairy godmothers looked at one another.

'What?' Cora asked.

'Someone's protecting you,' said Squash.

Protecting me? Instinctively, she pulled her arm away, covering the white chain. Dot had asked her once about the bracelet. Cora had thought she had given it to her. But Dot said it was with her the day she found her. Cora had never taken it off.

'Well, they're doing a terrible job,' said Cora, thinking of the Jinx.

'Now, stand still,' said Squeak.

Cora stood as still as she could.

The fairy godmothers flew in front of her. Then one of them pointed a finger at her. There was a *POP!* and Cora waited. Nothing happened. Suddenly, she felt a little funny in her tummy. Then she hiccupped. And hiccupped. And hiccupped again.

'Do you feel less cursed?' asked Tock.

Cora shook her head. She felt the same but with hiccups.

'Drink this,' said one of the fairies, handing her a cup of tea. Cora sniffed it. It smelt terrible. She blocked her nose and sipped it. *Bleugh!* It tasted like dirt and leaves.

'What is this?' Cora spluttered, shrinking away from it.

'Dirt and leaves,' said the old fairy.

Instantly, Cora's hiccups were gone.

'Sometimes magic has side effects,' said Squeak. Then she pointed a finger at her and there was another *POP!*

Cora suddenly felt her arm start to itch. And then she felt itchy all over. She scratched every part of her.

There was a *POP!* and the itching stopped but this time Cora felt something tickling her ears. She turned to a mirror near her and watched as a steady stream of bubbles floated out of her ears.

Tick and Tock smiled widely at her.

There was a *POP!* and the bubbles were gone.

'Oh, but that could have been useful,' said Tick, disappointed.

'The Jinx might be scared of bubbles,' said Tock.

Then from outside, somewhere in the distance, there was a loud crash followed by an earth-shaking shudder.

Tick's and Tock's smiles disappeared.

The fairy godmothers stopped their magic.

Then the whole room shuddered. Everything shook around them. The teacups in the cabinet bounced on their shelves. The floor and the roof trembled. Then the teacups smashed. And furniture fell.

The fairy godmothers looked towards the window but Cora knew what it was. She looked at Tick and Tock. They knew what it was too.

They had run out of time.

The Jinx had found her.

Chapter Eighteen

Cora felt like she couldn't breathe. It was here. The Jinx was back. What were they going to do? What was *she* going to do?

'I thought you said we had a few days,' Cora said to Tick and Tock in a panic.

'That was an estimate,' said Tock.

'A very rough estimate,' added Tick.

'More like a guess, really,' said Tock.

'Never mind,' interrupted Squeak.

'You need to get out of here,' said Squash. She grabbed Cora's pack and coat and handed them both to her.

Then the old fairies quickly ushered her out of the hut with Tick and Tock following. When they opened the door and stepped outside, they stopped in horror at what they saw.

Huts were smashed apart; their intricate branches lay broken and splintered in pieces. The lights that lit up the village in a beautiful glow were shattered on the ground. Smoke and debris covered the valley. The fairy village was completely destroyed.

'We need to find the king,' said Tock and with a *POP!*, he and Tick were gone.

'Listen,' said Squeak. 'Follow the path back into the forest.' She straightened her glasses determinedly on her nose.

'There's a gateway there,' said Squash. She adjusted her nightcap on her head resolutely. 'We'll hold it off.'

'But, you can't —' Cora tried, but with two more *POP!s*, the fairy godmothers were gone.

Cora stood there by herself. She looked out at the destruction ahead of her. Then from amongst the wreckage, Cora saw the creature emerge. It lumbered through the valley like a moving wall of shadow. She ignored the tingling of her bracelet as she watched fairies fly around the Jinx. Some fairies flew at the creature and were easily swatted out of its path. She heard *POP!s* of magic as some fairies tried to stop the creature. The valley echoed with shouts and cries.

A sharp pain entered Cora's chest. *This is because of me.* She had done this. She had brought the Jinx to the fairy kingdom. She needed to do something to help. But what? She remembered what happened to her in Urt, when she had locked eyes with the shadowy creature and couldn't move. It wouldn't be long until the Jinx saw her and then she would be powerless to stop it.

As she stared up at the creature, she saw it sniff the air. It was looking for her. Cora tried to think. The fairy godmothers had said there was a gateway nearby. She looked at the path that led away from the hut and up the hill into the forest. But if she left, the Jinx would just follow her to the next place she went to. And the next. And the next place after that. How many people would get hurt because of her? And how many homes would get destroyed?

The pain in Cora's chest turned into anger. She thought about Dot and Scratch. She thought about their home. She wasn't going to let anybody else get hurt because of her. The Jinx was here. And if it wanted her, it could have her.

Cora took a deep breath and screamed at the top of her lungs. She waved her hands high in the air. And then without waiting to check if the Jinx had seen her, Cora turned and ran. She ran away from the village and away from the path that led to the gateway. Instead, she ran towards the lake.

Gripping her pack, she raced down the sloping path. On the other side of the valley there weren't any lights to guide her way. Cora stumbled and fell but she got up quickly and kept going.

Was it following her?

Then she heard the familiar thundering steps behind her. She felt the ground shake beneath her feet as she ran.

It was.

Without looking over her shoulder, Cora heard the Jinx lumber through the village in her direction. She pushed through the tall grass and jumped over logs. She tried to focus on what was ahead of her: the lake.

When she got to the shore, Cora stopped. She hadn't thought this through. What now? Heart beating fast, she looked around for something to get her across. Then she spotted a small boat on the bank ahead. She raced towards it. With a grunt and a groan, she pushed the boat out into the lake. The water was cold and she bit back a cry as the icy wetness touched her legs. Holding the boat steady, she jumped inside it. Then with her back to the village, she grabbed the paddle at the bottom of the boat and paddled as fast as she could out into the lake.

The boat dipped as she heard the thundering shake of the Jinx's steps get closer. The water in the lake rippled and the boat rocked in waves. She paddled through them. She wasn't sure how far out into the lake she was. It was dark all around her, the water barely glistening in the moonlight.

It won't be long now, Cora thought. The Jinx was surely close.

Cora stopped paddling. She was about to place her paddle down when, suddenly, the rippling and shaking in the lake slowed. Cora glanced around.

Huh?

Cora knew that if she turned around, she might not be able to move again. She waited to hear the Jinx's steps. She waited some more. But they never came.

Have the fairies stopped it?

She closed her eye and took a deep breath. Then she used her paddle to turn the boat around. When she thought she was facing the village, she opened her eye.

In front of her, the Jinx stood on the edge of the lake, unmoving.

It stared out at her with its burning, yellow eyes.

Cora didn't understand. Why wasn't it moving? Why wasn't it coming for her?

The Jinx continued to stand still on the shore.

Is it asleep? she wondered.

Then Cora remembered what Tock had said earlier about Jinxes and bubbles. Her heart leapt.

The water!

Jinxes hate water! That had to be it. She had found a weakness! Cora couldn't believe it.

Then the Jinx placed one foot into the lake. And then the other.

Crud.

Chapter Nineteen

ora could only watch as the Jinx walked through
the lake towards her. She couldn't have moved
even if she had wanted to. She was frozen in place
as she stared into the burning, yellow eyes of the Jinx.
Slow step after slow step, the creature lumbered closer.
Soon it was almost halfway across the lake.

This is it, Cora thought.

She thought about the fairies. She thought about
Tick and Tock, and how much they had tried to help
her. She hoped they were okay. She hoped that all the
fairies in the kingdom were okay. Even King Clang.

The Jinx pushed its way through the water, sinking
lower as it walked along the deepening lake floor. The
water sloshed upwards, coming to a stop at its waist.

Cora felt the boat rock beneath her as the Jinx
approached, her eye still locked on its burning, yellow
eyes. And then she smelt it. The thick smell of ash
and burning wood filled her nostrils. For a minute,

she thought it was coming from the fairy kingdom. That something was on fire. But then she realised that the smell was actually coming from the Jinx. The shadowy creature smelt of ash and smoke.

Cora wondered how it was going to happen. Would the Jinx swallow her whole? Would it take bites? Would they be big bites or small bites? Would she be seasoned?

Then the Jinx came to a stop in the lake in front of her.

Cora's boat was tossed in the waves. She stared up at the creature. From up close, Cora could make out two rows of sharp teeth jutting out from its mouth, and a bulbous nose sitting in the middle of the shadowy darkness of its face. She swallowed. She hoped she at least tasted good.

The Jinx paused as it looked down at her. Then, as if in slow motion, one of its large hands reached down towards the boat.

Cora watched as the hand descended upon her. She thought about her family. About Dot and Scratch. She saw their faces one last time.

The Jinx's fingers wrapped around her, grabbing her tightly in its fist. It felt like she was being hugged by a cold mist at first and then the Jinx's grip tightened. *Very* tight. Cora's bracelet tingled on her skin. Then the Jinx's shadow fingers continued to tighten themselves around her. She wasn't able to breathe. She tried to break free. She felt her feet leave the boat as the Jinx lifted her up into the air. She pushed against the creature's hand with all her might. It felt like she was pushing against a wall.

Then, suddenly, Cora felt a shock go through her entire body. It sparked and sizzled like a bolt of lightning ricocheting from her toes to her nose. Cora closed her eye. She tingled all over. It felt like an energy from somewhere was filling her up.

Wait. How was she able to close her eye? The Jinx had her. She shouldn't have been able to move. Then she felt strength in her arms and her legs. She squirmed in the Jinx's grasp. She could move again! Not only that, she felt … something else.

She opened her eye and saw that she was still in the air. But the Jinx's hand didn't feel like a wall anymore. She pushed hard against the creature's hold. The Jinx's fingers began to move and then suddenly Cora broke free from the creature's grasp.

She fell through the air out of the Jinx's hand and then with a clunk, she landed back down in the boat. It pitched about in the water with the force of her fall.

'Ow,' Cora rubbed her back where she'd landed. Then sitting up, she looked around her, eye wide. How had she done that?

The Jinx pulled its arm back. It looked from its hand back down to where Cora sat in the boat and back to its hand again.

Cora sprang up. She felt … strange. Like she could lift a house. She tried to ignore the feeling that bubbled inside her as she watched the Jinx stare down at her.

Then with its hand, the shadowy creature reached down towards her again.

Cora didn't know what to do. She was in a boat in the middle of a lake. She couldn't run. She couldn't hide. Then at her feet, she spotted the paddle. She picked it up and just as the Jinx's hand was about to grab her again, she batted it away as hard as she could with the wooden paddle.

It struck the Jinx with a *CRACK!* and the creature went flying backwards through the water. It was like it had been hit by something that definitely wasn't an eleven-year-old girl. The creature came to a skidding stop in the middle of the lake, a large wave crashing onto the shore behind it.

WHOA!

Cora looked down at her hands, shocked at her sudden strength.

Then the Jinx sat up in the middle of the lake. If it wasn't happy before, it definitely didn't look happy now. Then, standing, the creature lumbered straight towards her once more.

Uh-oh.

Cora thought quickly. *Focus*, she told herself. Maybe she could use her strange strength again. She gripped onto the paddle in her hands. She couldn't wait for the Jinx to reach her. What if she swung and missed it? Then carefully, she took aim at the creature ahead as it sped towards her. She hefted the paddle back, closed her eye and then with a cry, she hurled it as hard as she could at the Jinx.

The paddle soared through the night like a spear. It went straight into the creature and out the other side, dispersing its shadow into many. The shadows floated up into the night air and then with a shudder, the Jinx disappeared.

Cora looked out onto the empty lake in amazement. Breathing heavily, she looked down at her hands again unable to comprehend how she had defeated the beast. The strange feeling inside her was still there.

Then Cora felt a wave of dizziness hit her. She put a hand to her head. The lake around her began to spin. The boat beneath her feet rolled from side to side. She fell backwards. Just as she was about to hit the deck, she heard two *POP!s* nearby. Then there was nothing but darkness.

Chapter Twenty

Cora heard two voices. They floated in the air around her like a dream.

'Maybe she is an ogre?' suggested one of the voices.

'She doesn't look like any of the ogres we've seen,' said the other voice.

'Maybe she's a shape-shifter?' replied the first voice. 'An ogre shape-shifter.'

'Or maybe it was just … luck,' said the second voice.

She was lying on something soft. Was it a bed? Or cushions? It felt comfortable. She kept her eye closed as she listened.

'Luck?' echoed the first voice. 'She hit a Jinx halfway across a lake. You saw it with your own eyes. We both did.'

As she lay there, Cora suddenly realised that she wasn't dreaming at all. Flashes of memory flooded her mind. She remembered the fairy kingdom completely destroyed. She remembered running to the lake and paddling out. She remembered the Jinx grabbing her. She remembered not being able to breathe. Then she remembered feeling strange and the Jinx disappearing.

Somehow, she had faced the Jinx and survived. Then she recognised the two voices floating around her. They belonged to Tick and Tock. She'd thought she would never see the fairies again.

'Maybe she *is* a witch,' said Tick.

Cora couldn't help herself. 'I'm *not* a witch,' she said as she opened her eye. She stared up at Tick and Tock with a smile.

The fairies flew down to her, surprised.

'You're alive!' said Tick, clasping his hands together. '*How* are you alive?'

Tock elbowed the fairy. 'What he means to say is that we are so happy you are alive.'

'Yes,' said Tick, rubbing his side, 'we knew you could do it.'

The fairies helped Cora as she sat up slowly. She looked around her. They were in an empty room. Beneath her sat a bed of cushions on a wooden floor. Daylight shone through a small window opposite.

'We have a few questions,' said Tock.

'So do I,' mumbled Cora.

'One: *how* are you alive?' asked Tick.

Cora smiled.

'How do you feel?' asked Tock, shooting a look at Tick.

'Sore,' she said, rubbing her back. 'Tired.' And she still felt that strange feeling inside. It bubbled beneath the surface. Cora pushed it aside.

'Where are we?' she asked.

'We're in a house,' said Tock. 'And we are somewhat sure nobody lives here.'

'Somewhat sure?' Cora questioned.

Tick and Tock nodded.

'Where is this house?' Cora asked. Were they still in The Hollow? It didn't look like it.

'Gwell,' said Tock.

Cora had never heard of a place called Gwell. But Cora hadn't heard of many places.

'It's a small town way away from The Hollow,' explained Tock.

'And far away from Urt,' added Tick.

'When did we get here?' she asked.

'Day before yesterday,' said Tick.

'And before here we were in Tranthia and before Tranthia we were in Orris —'

'Wait,' interrupted Cora, trying to understand. 'When were we at these places?' She tried to think back to them. Her head pounded softly in her ears. 'I–I don't remember.'

'Oh, you won't remember them,' said Tock.

'You have been asleep for two days,' said Tick.

'What?' replied Cora, shocked. *Two days!*

Tick and Tock nodded at her.

'It gave us time,' said Tock. 'And we have a plan.' He puffed out his chest confidently.

'With the Jinx no longer on our tails ...' said Tick.

'… we were able to magic you to different places,' said Tock.

'He won't know where to start looking for you,' said Tick, proudly. 'But after what you did, he may not be back for a little while.'

Then Cora realised something. What *had* happened to the Jinx? Was it over? 'Is it … did I …?' she stammered.

'Oh, the Jinx isn't dead,' said Tock. 'Just injured and angry.'

Cora groaned. For the briefest of moments she thought she would be able to go back to Urt and look for Dot. That she was no longer cursed. That she had defeated the Jinx.

'Just like King Clang is injured and angry with us,' said Tick.

Cora looked up at the fairies apologetically. Part of her was glad they were way away from The Hollow. She couldn't think of facing the rest of the fairies after what she had done to their kingdom.

'I-I'm sorry,' she said to Tick and Tock. 'About The Hollow.'

Tick and Tock shook their heads.

'We thought we had more time,' said Tock.

'Are the fairies … is everyone okay?' she asked, afraid to hear the answer. Slowly, she stood up from where she sat. Her bones ached as she moved them. Tick and Tock watched her carefully.

'They will be fine,' said Tock, with a wave of his hand.

'The Hollow will be rebuilt in no time,' said Tick, a small smile on his lips.

With a shuffle, Cora walked over to the window in the room. Looking out it, she could see a busy village outside. She was surprised the fairies were still helping her after what had happened. Why *were* they still helping her?

'Why are you here?' she asked, turning around. 'With me? Why aren't you back there helping your people?'

'We got you into this mess,' said Tick, looking down.

'We are going to get you out,' said Tock.

Tick nodded. 'And this is the most excitement we've had in years.'

Cora stared at the fairies. There was something they weren't saying. Then, under her gaze, the fairies looked to their feet.

'Besides … King Clang …' said Tick, trailing off.

'He kind of … sort of …' continued Tock.

'Won't … let us back,' finished Tick.

'What?' gasped Cora.

'We've been banished,' said Tock.

The guilt hit Cora like a thunderbolt. 'You can't go back … because of me?' Not only had she destroyed The Hollow, but she had also destroyed any chance that the fairies could go back. 'For forever?'

'Well, we can't go back because of us,' said Tock.

'King Clang will calm down in a few years,' said Tick.

'A few years?!' exclaimed Cora.

Tick and Tock nodded.

Cora closed her eye. 'You should have just left me in Urt,' she mumbled.

'Left you?' asked Tock.

'You faced a Jinx and are still alive!' said Tick.

'It's unheard of!'

'It's unbelievable!'

'I–I don't know what that was,' Cora said, looking away. 'One minute I–I couldn't breathe and then the next minute I could. I could breathe and feel everything. I felt … strong.'

Tick and Tock shared a look.

'What?' asked Cora.

'It's time for the next part of our plan,' said Tock with a smile.

'The next part?' she asked.

'To hide your scent,' said Tick.

'We can do that?'

'Maybe,' said Tock.

Cora wasn't filled with much confidence.

Then the fairies flew towards her, touched her on the shoulder and with a *POP!*, the three of them were gone.

Chapter Twenty-One

*C*ora opened her eye to find herself on a dry, empty road. The wind whipped up around her. Tick and Tock fluttered nearby. Opposite them, on the other side of the road sat a small store with a red door. Above the red door swung a sign with the words *Bits and Bobs*. Cora thought the store looked like it could have belonged in Urt. It was completely rundown and forgotten.

'Where are we?' she asked. Cora squinted into the sun. She could see a village not far away. The dry, empty road she stood on wound all the way from the village and continued onwards, past them and up along the dry earth ahead into the distance.

'The Black Market of Gwell,' said Tock.

Cora didn't see any market at all. 'Are you sure this is the right place?'

'I think so,' said Tick, scratching his head.

Then the red door of the store in front of them

opened and a man stepped out. Cora panicked. She was standing with two flying fairies in broad daylight. What if he saw them?

But the man, who wore a hat and a cloak, didn't even look up. He kept his head down, walked down the road and then suddenly, he shimmered … and disappeared. Cora stared at where the man had been just a moment earlier.

'Did he just …?'

'Yep,' said Tock. 'This is the right place.'

They crossed the road to the Bits and Bobs store. The store looked even more rundown up close. The wood was rotten and the red paint on the door was peeling off around the edges. A sign sat behind a broken window.

Gwellcome, it read.

Tock pushed open the red door with a creak. A small bell attached to it chimed as they entered. Inside, it was dark. Cora noticed that they were the only ones in the store besides a small man who sat on a high stool behind the counter. He didn't look up from the newspaper he was reading.

Placed carefully on the shelves along the walls sat all sorts of … bits and bobs. Toys, books, clothes, furniture, rugs. Cora had never seen such a collection all in one place. If she had stumbled on a store like this back in Urt, she would have needed to make ten trips to carry it all home.

I wish you could see this, Dot.

Cora walked up to the nearest shelf. She ran her hand along it and a layer of thick, grey dust stuck to her fingers. She picked up a hairbrush with a silver handle and coughed as some of the dust flew up her nose. It was like none of the bits and bobs had been touched in … years.

Tick and Tock flew over to the shelf beside her.

'This must be the market,' said Tock, picking up a small, pink doll's house.

Cora looked at the fairy. Had he not seen a doll's house before?

Tock opened the doors on the doll's house and stared inside it. Cora could see small chairs and a bed inside. She waited. And as she suspected, nothing happened.

'Nope,' said Tock putting the doll's house back on the shelf.

'This must be it,' said Tick, holding up a dusty shoe. He held it up high and stared into it. Cora waited. And again nothing happened.

'What are you two doing?' she asked, confused and slightly concerned.

'We're looking for the door to the Black Market,' said Tock, as he held up a hat and looked inside it.

'It's hidden,' said Tick, looking inside a vase.

'The market is hidden inside a vase?' Cora replied disbelievingly.

'It could be anywhere,' said Tick, opening a glass jar. 'Even in here.'

'The Black Market is charmed,' said Tock, grabbing and unfurling a dress from the shelf.

Cora sneezed as more dust flew up into the air in a plume.

'So that it can't be found by just anyone,' said Tock, peering into a mirror that sat on the wall. Then he paused and made a face. Nothing.

'The fairy godmothers said it could be anything. Even something small,' said Tick, shoving the dress back onto the shelf.

'This must be it,' said Tock, picking up a thimble. He peered inside it. They waited. Nothing.

Cora stepped away from the fairies. She looked around her for something that could be hiding the market. But there were so many things. She picked up a wooden doll that sat on the shelf. Dust whirled up into her mouth and eye. She coughed and spluttered. 'Everything is so dusty,' she said, fanning it away with a hand. Then Cora had an idea. The items in the shop were all dusty because they weren't ever used. Which meant …

'We need to find something that isn't dusty,' she whispered. She walked over to one of the shelves opposite them. She scanned the items. Dusty. She moved to the next shelf. Everything had a thick layer of dust. They hadn't been touched.

Then on the back wall of the store Cora's eye spotted a small jewellery box sitting on a shelf by itself. She walked over to it and saw straight away that it wasn't like the rest of the things in the store. It wasn't dusty. Her heart leapt.

Carefully, Cora picked up the jewellery box. She ran her hand along the top of the round lid. It was old. Its pink and gold colours were long faded. On its side, she saw that its winder was bent. Cora tried to picture the jewellery box when it was once a bright pink and a shining gold. Even old and broken as it was, Dot would have loved it.

Cora lifted the lid. A soft tune floated out of the round box. On the other side of the lid was a painting of a castle, and in the centre of the box, a princess in a long, gold dress twirled on the spot. Then suddenly Cora felt herself being tugged forward.

She gasped. The jewellery box shook in her hands. Alarmed, Cora tried to put the box back but it was stuck to her hand. Cora couldn't pull away from it. Something was pulling her inside the box, towards the painting of the castle. It got stronger and stronger. Then her feet lifted off the ground.

'Ahh!' she cried out. She tried to call out to Tick and Tock but it was too late. With a *SLURP!* her whole body was sucked into the jewellery box.

Chapter Twenty-Two

Cora felt herself stretching, like she was made of elastic. First her head, then her shoulders, her torso and her legs. They all twisted and stretched as she spun around. She didn't know which way was up. And then as quickly as it happened, it was over. With a soft *clunk*, Cora's boots hit the ground. She opened her eye and saw that she was on pavement instead of a store floor. And instead of being surrounded by shelves of bits and bobs, she was surrounded by a big, dimly lit marketplace.

In front of her were shops. Dark, stone shop fronts lined up in a row. Like the traders in Urt, the shops sat on both sides of the paved road and lamps shone a murky light on the street outside the front of them. People skulked down the road and ducked in and out of the shops, their heads down.

'I guess this is the market,' Cora said to herself.

She turned around. Behind her was a brick wall

and painted on it was the same picture of the castle that was on the jewellery box.

Then with a *SLURP!* the painting shimmered. Tick and Tock flew through the painting and straight into her. The three of them crashed to the ground in a heap of legs and arms and wings.

'You did it!' said Tick.

'I really thought it would be the doily,' said Tock, disappointed.

The fairies flew upwards and lifted Cora with them. Carefully, they placed her back on her feet and then landed on the ground themselves.

'Right,' said Tick, rubbing his hands together. 'Where shall we start?'

The fairies looked ahead of them. A man five times their size approached them. Cora took a step backwards. The man peered down at them. He had a small beard that ran across his square chin. Tick and Tock looked up at him.

'You're blocking the door,' he said in a deep voice.

Quickly, Cora and the fairies stepped away from the painting on the wall.

'Apologies,' said Tick.

The man grunted and walked towards the wall. Then the painting shimmered and he was gone.

'Let's not dilly or dally,' said Tock, with a shudder. 'People here might not be as friendly.'

Cora wasn't sure she liked the sound of that.

The three of them walked along the paved road. Cora looked inside the first shop window they came to. Inside it were candles of all kinds of shapes, sizes and colours. They were alight with blue flames and spun in the air on their own. Then one by one they were snuffed out only to alight once more seconds later. She didn't think they needed candles. But then again she wasn't exactly sure what they needed.

'What are we looking for?' Cora asked as they walked past the candle shop.

Tick and Tock shrugged.

The next shop they came to had bones dangling in the window. Cora grimaced. Tick and Tock shook their heads.

'Nope,' said Tock and the three of them moved down the paved road.

They walked past a shop window that had three mannequins dressed in capes. The store didn't seem too bad. Cora pictured herself wearing one. Then suddenly the capes on the mannequins burst into flames. Cora jumped back.

'Combustible capes,' said Tock.

'They were popular a few years ago,' said Tick.

'Until they burnt everybody,' added Tock.

'Then they became very *un*popular,' said Tick.

The shops at the market definitely weren't like any Cora had ever seen before. Next to them, a woman came out of the store. She stopped when she saw them before pushing past down the road.

'Not a very cheerful place,' mumbled Cora. In a way, it reminded her of Urt.

Ahead of them, two people walked down the paved road. As they walked by, the man and woman stared at them. Then opposite, a young man came out of a shop, his eyes on them before he quickly scuttled off down the road. Why was everyone looking at them like that?

Cora turned and then through a shop window, she saw an older woman peering out at them.

'Are we allowed to be here?' Cora asked as they walked.

'Definitely not,' said Tock, also noticing the eyes on them.

'The Black Market of Gwell is hidden for a reason,' said Tick.

Cora's stomach lurched.

'And fairies aren't particularly welcome,' said Tock.

'Why?' asked Cora.

'Neither are children,' added Tick.

Cora groaned. She pulled the hood of her coat up and over her head.

The next shop they walked past had cages in the window. Inside the cages were jumping spiders with very long legs.

'Let me guess,' said a voice to their left. Cora, Tick and Tock turned to find a woman standing by the door of a shop behind them. She was hunched over and her long, black hair fell past her shoulders. She leant on a walking stick.

'You need an eye,' the woman finished. 'We only have troll eyes left.' She cackled loudly revealing sharp, yellowing teeth.

The three of them looked at her, confused.

The woman stopped cackling and then annoyed, pointed to Cora.

'Oh, ah, no, thank you,' said Cora. She shuddered at the thought of having a troll eye. What would a troll eye even look like?

'We need something to hide her scent,' said Tock.

'From a werewolf?' the woman asked.

Cora swallowed. *Werewolf?!*

'A Jinx,' said Tick.

The woman nodded. She looked at Cora. 'Pity,' she said. Then she turned and entered her shop. Cora glanced inside the window of the woman's shop but black curtains covered every inch of it. She looked at Tick and Tock. They shrugged. Cora wondered if the woman could help them. She didn't say she couldn't. Without another thought, Cora walked across the paved road and followed the lady into her shop.

Chapter Twenty-Three

When she entered, Cora wasn't surprised to see that the inside of the shop was just as darkly lit as it seemed from the outside. Each corner of the room was filled with unusual items she definitely couldn't have found at a trader's stall in Urt. Glowing crystals sat in baskets at her feet, chimes made up of charred animal bones dangled from above and small, black cauldrons billowed small puffs of smoke nearby. Cora peered into a cabinet lined with what looked like plaits of woven human hair. Next to it was a shelf of toenails, each of them a different size, shape and tinge of yellow.

Why would somebody want to buy somebody else's toenails? she wondered, a little disgusted.

Tick and Tock peered into a large round bowl that sat opposite her. Something squelchy slithered around inside it.

'Lizard guts,' said the woman.

Tick and Tock recoiled.

Cora walked over to a tray and picked up what looked like a handful of dried leaves.

'Dried bat tongues,' said the woman.

Cora dropped them instantly.

The woman cleared her throat loudly and moved to the back of the shop.

'Nothing here will help you,' she said. 'Not from a Jinx.'

The hope Cora had briefly felt was suddenly snuffed out like one of the candles in the first shop window.

They watched as the woman then turned, pushed aside the black curtains at the back of the shop and entered another part of the store.

Tick, Tock and Cora looked at each other.

'I think she wants us to follow her,' said Tick, unsure.

There was a pause.

'I do,' came the woman's voice from the other side of the curtains.

Tick, Tock and Cora walked to the back of the shop and pulled aside the black curtains. Behind them sat another, smaller room that was darker than the first. It was dimly lit by candles grouped in threes and fours. Glancing up, Cora saw symbols carved onto the ceiling. They glowed like stars in the night.

There were piles of large, heavy-bound books and opened drawers filled with neatly placed jewellery. Cora looked down at what she thought was a gold and red bracelet … until it sat up and scurried across the drawer. The woman quickly grabbed hold of the bracelet and put it back in its original spot.

Tick and Tock walked over to an open drawer filled with colourful stones while Cora made her way over to a tall shelf stacked high with glass jars in the corner of the room. The jars were different shapes and sizes. The first jar had a thick, brown liquid inside it. It looked kind of like mud. The next had a yellow paste inside it that moved around the sides of the jar like a slug. The third jar was round and filled with small, green legs.

Frogs' legs? Cora wondered. They twitched in the jar. Cora grimaced. Next to the frogs' legs was a large jar filled with bright green and red eyeballs. Cora stopped.

'Troll eyes,' she gasped. The eyeballs were huge. They were almost the size of her hand.

With a finger, Cora tapped lightly on the glass jar. Then suddenly all of the eyes rolled around to look at her.

'Ahh!' she cried out, jumping backwards in surprise.

The woman cackled loudly as Cora quickly backed away from the shelf of jars. The eyes followed her.

The woman walked over to the large, locked cabinet on the far wall. It was almost as tall and wide as the room. Cora watched as the woman pulled a small, gold key on a chain from around her neck and unlocked the cabinet. The woman opened up the doors wide.

Inside the cabinet lay a selection of sharply pointed knives, maces, bow and arrows, sickles and even a sword. Cora swallowed as she looked at the deadly collection of items in front of her.

Tick and Tock walked over to the cabinet, too.

'The Jinx curse is very powerful,' said the woman. Then she picked up something shiny from the cabinet. She turned and showed them. It was a small dagger.

'What's that for?' Cora asked worriedly.

'My nails,' said the woman as though it were obvious. She started to clean her nails with the sharp knife.

'For the Jinx you'll need something like this perhaps,' said the woman once she had finished with her nails. She pulled open a drawer that lay inside the cabinet and pulled out a jar filled with thick, green liquid. The liquid popped and sizzled in the jar. 'It will need to be drunk at least six times a day. Side effects include boils, pustules, blisters and excessive armpit hair. It's usually used to ward off ghosts but it *could* work on a Jinx.'

Tick and Tock looked at Cora.

Cora imagined herself covered in boils, pustules and blisters and growing excessive armpit hair. She shook her head.

Then Cora spotted a small, gold necklace that sat near her and picked it up. 'What about this?' she suggested. It looked harmless. And she wouldn't need to drink it.

The woman nodded. 'You could try it,' she said. Then she smiled her yellow, toothy smile. 'But you will need to bathe in the blood springs first.'

Cora put down the necklace.

'What about this?' asked Tock, holding up a bright red stone. It glimmered in the candlelight.

'That only works on babies,' said the woman.

Tick looked at Cora, squinting.

'I'm not a baby,' she said.

Tick nodded.

'Perhaps this,' said the woman. She held up what looked to Cora like an oddly shaped potato.

'What is it?' Cora asked. She hoped she didn't have to eat it, although it did look more edible than the thick, green, popping, sizzling liquid.

'Whisper root,' said the woman. 'Rare. We only have one left.'

'What do you do with it?' Cora tried to picture herself using it against the Jinx. Would she throw it at it? Feed it to it? Leave it somewhere for the Jinx to trip over?

'You must burn it and cover yourself in its smoke,' said the woman. 'It won't last but it will help cover your scent for a short amount of time … or so I hear.'

Cora looked at Tick and Tock. It sounded easy enough. She reached out her hand as the woman offered her the oddly-shaped potato. As she grabbed hold of it, Cora's coat sleeve moved up and the woman's eyes glanced down at her wrist. Cora took the oddly shaped potato and quickly covered her bracelet again with the sleeve of her coat.

The woman looked back at her, intrigued.

'Do you know what that is?' she asked, pointing to Cora's wrist with her knife.

Cora remembered what the fairy godmothers had said. 'It's … for protection.'

The woman nodded. 'It's made from ice stone. A very powerful material. Often used for protection from others.' The woman paused. 'And sometimes used for protection from oneself.'

'Oneself?' Cora echoed. Why would she need to be protected from herself?

The woman nodded. 'I can take it off your hands,' she said, her eyes gleaming in the dim candlelight.

Tick and Tock came to stand by Cora.

'If you know that it's ice stone …' said Tick.

'… then you know it can't be removed,' said Tock.

'It can't?' asked Cora, looking at them. She pulled back her coat sleeve and looked down at the white chain on her wrist. She tried to remember if she had ever taken it off. She hadn't.

'There are ways,' said the woman, with a shrug.

There was something about her expression that made Cora never want to find out what those ways were.

'Do you want the whisper root or not?' the woman asked, impatiently.

Cora nodded. Perhaps it would be enough. At least for a little while. At least until she could figure out what to do. The strange feeling she felt at The Hollow still bubbled beneath her skin.

The woman closed up her cabinet and made her way out of the room. Cora, Tick and Tock followed. They pushed aside the black curtains and stopped in their tracks. A man stood in the middle of the brightly lit store. His dark hair was grey at the sides, long and untidy. His mouth curved downwards into a grim line.

Archibald Drake.

Chapter Twenty-Four

Archibald Drake turned his gaze away from a jar of enormously sharp teeth and looked over at them. Cora, Tick and Tock stared back. Cora's bracelet tingled at her wrist. Her stomach squirmed as the warlock's dark eyes rested on her and his mouth curved upwards into a strange smile that stretched slowly across his thin face.

Crud.

In the air beside her, she felt Tick and Tock move closer towards her. Archibald must have noticed it too because annoyance coloured the man's face.

'Smelda,' he said to the woman. 'You're not serving *fairies* and *children*, are you?'

Cora gulped. She remembered what Tick and Tock had said about the Black Market. Fairies and children *weren't* welcome.

The woman faltered. 'I ... uh ...' she said. 'I was just telling them to leave.'

'You cannot follow rules, can you?' Archibald spat. 'This is exactly the sort of behaviour that forced the witches to cast you out.'

The woman looked away.

Cora clutched the whisper root in her hand. The woman was just trying to help her. Suddenly the feeling she felt in The Hollow, the one she had been pushing aside since she woke up in Gwell, bubbled to the surface.

Oh no.

'We were lost,' said Tock, hastily fishing a couple of coins out of his pocket and handing them to the shopkeeper.

'This strange woman was just telling us to leave,' said Tick.

Archibald stepped in front of them, blocking their path.

'Lost?' inquired Archibald.

Tick and Tock nodded.

'You accidentally opened the charmed jewellery box that brought you here?' he asked.

'We were in the market for one,' said Tock.

'A jewellery box?'

Tick nodded. 'They're very pretty.'

Archibald stared at the fairies. Cora could see that he didn't believe a word they were saying. A small bell tinkled and through the door two men entered the shop. Archibald turned around to look behind him at the two men.

Cora breathed a small sigh of relief. *A distraction.* The fairies could use their magic to get them out of the market while the warlock wasn't looking.

'Do your magic,' she whispered to Tick and Tock out of the side of her mouth.

'We can't,' whispered Tock.

'Why not?'

'Fairy magic doesn't work in here. There's only one way in and one way out,' whispered Tick.

Cora groaned. *The painting.* How would they get past Archibald?

In front of her, the men locked eyes with Archibald. They spun around and left the shop the way they came, the small bell tinkling after them.

Cora's stomach dropped. They were trapped in a room with a warlock and a witch. And the only way out was the way they had come in. She fought the feeling that gripped her. She felt like she needed to scream. Like she needed to let something go. She took a few deep breaths.

No, no, no. She tried to push it down.

'Are you alright?' Tock asked.

Cora felt her hands begin to shake.

'Now,' Archibald began, turning to them, 'where were we? Oh, yes!' His eyes settled on Cora. 'You.'

'Me?' Cora replied.

'I know what you are,' he said, taking a step forward.

'People would,' he paused before smiling, '*kill* to have what you have.'

Cora swallowed. She didn't like the way Archibald stared at her. His eyes shone with greed. *He knows what I am? What am I?*

'You are coming with me,' he growled.

'No,' Cora blurted out. It came out louder than she had meant it to.

A noise had started to pound in her ears.

Archibald tilted his head at her, a surprised smile on his face. 'She speaks.'

Cora glared at the warlock.

'But,' he said, 'I don't remember asking.' Then Archibald raised a hand in front of him and Cora felt herself being pulled along the ground towards the warlock. She tried to fight it but her feet were dragged in front of her of their own will. She looked back at the fairies, wide-eyed.

Then Tick and Tock flew at the warlock. But Archibald was faster. He held up his other hand in front of him and both of the fairies suddenly froze in the air. Slowly, the warlock clenched his hand. And Tick and Tock screamed, their bodies twisting in pain as they hung suspended in the air.

'Stop it!' Cora cried out, horrified.

Then the warlock reached down and grabbed Cora's arm fiercely. She gasped. It hurt. Then the feeling she had had at The Hollow broke free. She couldn't stop it. It filled her up. Cora pushed the warlock as hard as she could and he flew up into the air and across the room, smashing through the shop window with a *CRASH!*

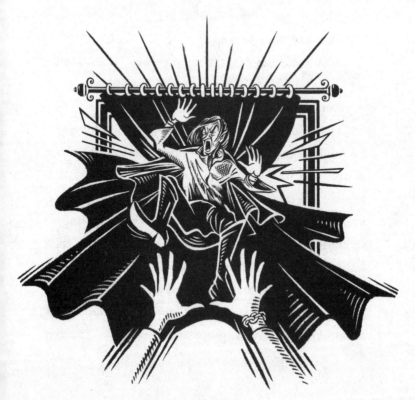

Cora stared open-mouthed.

The shop was quiet. Tick and Tock had stopped screaming. Cora looked up at them and was relieved to see that they were no longer twisting in pain. Their eyes were as wide as hers as they stared out the broken shop window. In a heap of glass and black curtains, Archibald Drake, warlock, lay on his back in the Black Market street.

Cora looked down at her hands. She still felt the strange feeling squirming beneath her skin. 'What's happening to me?' she gasped. Her head felt dizzy. The shop began to spin around her.

Tick and Tock looked down at her worriedly.

'Run,' said Smelda, the shop owner. 'Run. Now!' she said.

Cora couldn't think straight.

Tick and Tock flew down to Cora and pulled her by her coat towards the shop door. She stumbled out of the doorway with the fairies and into the Black Market street. Cora stopped and stared down at the unmoving warlock. *How did I do that?* Fear and unease sloshed around in her stomach like ingredients in a soup, making her feel sick.

Then up and down the market road, people and shop owners walked out of the stores on either side of them. Ahead of them, more and more people started filing into the street. They looked down at the man on the ground and then looked up at Cora.

'Hey!' a man in a dark suit called out to them. He pointed a finger towards Tick and Tock.

'Hurry ...' Tock said.

'... this way,' said Tick.

The fairies pulled Cora in the direction they had come in. They hurriedly pushed through the people that had gathered behind them on the paved road. Someone in the crowd tried to grab Cora but Tick and Tock tugged her harder.

Cora stumbled with the fairies until she had to run to keep up. Her head still felt dizzy. She reached a hand to her temple and realised she still held the whisper root.

Then more shouts came from behind them. Angry shouts. Tick, Tock and Cora raced down the paved road, away from the crowd. Cora looked behind her. A few people had started running after them. She tried her best not to fall over as she ran. But the ground wasn't staying still. It moved like water beneath her boots. She tried to focus on the fairies zipping ahead of her.

Then at last they could see the painting of the castle on the wall ahead. Cora panted as she ran. She felt the energy drain from her with each step.

Then suddenly there was a string of loud *POP! POP!s* near her. Someone was throwing magic at them!

They reached the painting of the castle. Tick and Tock flew through and without a second thought, Cora dived headfirst into the shimmering wall.

Chapter Twenty-Five

They landed on the Bits and Bobs shop floor. Cora groaned in pain. It felt like she had hit the wall instead of passing through it. She heard the buzz of fairy wings in her ears. She didn't want to get up from where she lay. She didn't think she could.

'Come on, Cora,' said Tock urgently.

There was a tug on her coat.

With the little strength she had left, Cora pulled herself upwards. She stood and tried to focus her vision. Standing in front of them was the shop owner. He was only as tall as she was and had bright red hair that stuck out every which way. The man stared back at them and crossed his arms over his chest.

'Let us pass, dwarf,' said Tick.

The dwarf glared at Tick. He wasn't going to let them pass. Cora knew that any minute now all sorts of magical beings were going to burst out of the jewellery box. All sorts of magical beings that were now after them. *Because of her.* She looked behind her and saw the jewellery box shake on the shelf. She could push past the dwarf but given what happened only moments ago, she didn't want to hurt anybody else. Then she remembered what Archibald had said.

'You let us in,' said Cora. 'Fairies and a child. You let us in.'

Tick and Tock folded their arms across their chests.

'When they find out …' said Tock.

'… boy, will you be in trouble,' finished Tick.

The small man stood still but Cora saw it. His eyes shifted worriedly. Then the dwarf stepped to the side.

Tick, Tock and Cora wasted no time. They raced past the dwarf and through the shop. Tick and Tock pushed open the door and the minute they were out of the shop, the fairies touched Cora on the arm, there was a loud *POP!* and then they were gone.

Cora opened her eye. Her head spun but she could see from the rock walls around her that she stood in a small cave. Glistening purple crystals sat nestled in the rock. They gave off a slight purple glow, lighting up the dark corners in a soft purple hue. Looking out of the cave opening, she could see the late afternoon sun was still out. She rested a hand on the wall behind her and closed her eye. She had thrown a warlock through a window! In broad daylight. In the Black Market of Gwell. A place filled with magical beings. She thought things were going from bad to worse before. Now things had gone from worse to even more worse.

'Cora,' Tick said softly.

She opened her eye to find Tick and Tock hovering in front of her, worry etched on their round faces.

'You need to rest,' said Tock.

Cora nodded.

The fairies walked her further into the cave and she sat down. Tick flew out of the cave and soon brought back a bundle of wood. Then with a *POP!* of magic, the wood was set alight and soon a fire burnt in front of them. There was silence for a while as the three of them stared into the fire, occupied with their own thoughts.

'What's happening to me?' Cora asked.

Tick and Tock looked at her across the fire.

'We don't know,' said Tick.

Cora was afraid of that.

'What happened at the Black Market?' asked Tock.

Cora closed her eye again. 'When … you were … in pain …' she said, not knowing what else to call

it, 'Archibald grabbed me on the arm and it hurt, so I … pushed him away … and …' she trailed off as she remembered the warlock flying through the window.

Tick and Tock looked at each other.

'He knows what you are,' said Tock.

'And that's not good,' said Tick.

'Wh-what am I?' Cora asked.

'We don't know that either,' said Tick.

'You could be many things,' said Tock.

Cora remembered what Archibald had said at Drake Manor. *That can mean … many things.* She just wanted an answer. Why couldn't anybody tell her?

'You could be an ogre,' said Tick.

'You could be a mage,' said Tock.

'You could be having a severe allergic reaction,' said Tick with a shrug.

Cora shook her head. She was certain that whatever was happening to her wasn't any of the things the fairies had mentioned. The feeling still squirmed beneath her skin.

'Whatever you are, we need to find out,' said Tock. 'And soon. Archibald will have already started looking for us.'

Cora groaned. 'Maybe he will just … forget about me?' she tried hopefully.

'Archibald is not going to quickly forget about being thrown through a wheelbarrow by a child,' said Tick.

'Window,' said Tock and Cora at the same time.

'Warlocks are very powerful magical beings,' said Tock. 'Especially Archibald Drake.'

This was not making Cora feel any better. She put her head in her hands. 'First the Jinx and now a very powerful warlock,' Cora mumbled.

'It could be worse,' said Tock.

Cora opened her eye and looked up. 'How?' She really could not see how it could be any worse.

'You could have taken that potion from the witch and be covered in boils and growing excessive armpit hair,' said Tick.

Cora gave the fairy a small smile. Perhaps it could have been worse.

There was a silence again as they stared into the fire. And then Cora whispered, 'I'm ... scared.'

'It will be okay,' said Tock.

'You have us,' said Tick. Smiling, he puffed out his chest. 'The best fairies in all the land.'

Cora gave him another small smile.

'Now we all need to rest,' said Tock. 'We'll figure out a plan in the morning.'

Cora hoped so. She felt her eye begin to close as she stared into the fire. The tiredness and dizziness she had been fighting had begun to take hold. She put down the whisper root she still held onto and lay down on the cave floor. She closed her eye. It wasn't long until Cora fell into a deep sleep.

Chapter Twenty-Six

*C*ora was in Urt. She gasped as she sprinted down an
  alleyway. She got to the end and skidded around the
  corner. Then she stopped. In front of her, standing in
the middle of the road, was Dot. She was holding Scratch in
her arms.

'Dot!' Cora cried. She ran up to her. But Dot's eyes
didn't meet hers. She watched as Dot pointed to something
behind Cora. She turned around. Charging down the road
towards them was the Jinx. The shadow creature moved
quickly; its yellow eyes on them. Both of its hands swiped
at the buildings either side of the road. Then it roared into
the air.

Cora turned back to Dot. 'Run!' she told her.

But Dot didn't move. Neither did Scratch.

'Dot! Run!' Cora called again. She realised that Dot
couldn't hear her. Cora waved her hands in front of the old
woman's face. And then she did the same in front of Scratch's
eyes. Nothing. They both remained still, staring up at the

*shadow creature. Cora looked over her shoulder. The Jinx
was getting closer.*

*Cora tried to push Dot off the road. But it was like she
was made of stone. She wouldn't budge. 'Please,' Cora urged
as she pushed as hard as she could. She felt her eye fill with
tears. 'Please move.'*

*The Jinx was almost on them. There seemed nothing
Cora could do. She stopped pushing and stood in front of Dot
and Scratch. It was all she could do. She faced the shadow
creature as it hurtled towards them. She closed her eye. Then
when she opened it again, she was looking down at Dot and
Scratch from up high. She raised her arms up and saw that
they were shadows. Then Cora reached down and grabbed
hold of Dot and Scratch. She lifted them up and held them
out in front of her. They tried to wriggle out of her grasp
but she opened her mouth wide and tossed them inside,
swallowing them whole in one big gulp.*

Cora sat up awake. Blinking, she realised she was still
inside the cave with the glowing purple stones from
the day before. Only now she was dripping with
water. *Huh?* She wiped her face and looked around.
Tick and Tock stared at her from the other side of
the fire.

'Are you okay?' asked Tock.

Cora nodded. Although she wasn't entirely sure she was. Dot's scared face still sat in her mind. Cora looked down. 'Why am I wet?' she asked.

'We thought you could be a mermaid,' said Tick.

'What? A mermaid?!' exclaimed Cora. The fairies sat cross-legged on the cave floor, each holding a notepad and pen in their hands, a pair of half-moon glasses atop their noses.

'We have already crossed off werewolf and soothsayer from the list, too,' said Tock.

'You didn't turn into a wolf last night and you have been doing a terrible job at predicting the future,' said Tick.

'Thank you?' Cora replied, unsure. She was glad to hear that she wasn't a werewolf or soothsayer. But she felt like she could have told them that.

'How do you feel?' asked Tick. He put down his notepad and handed her a small bowl.

'Better than yesterday,' she said. She looked down at the bowl in her hands. It was filled with a thick, white soup. Twigs floated along the top of it. 'What is this?'

'Why? Would you say you prefer blood?' asked Tock, pen poised on his notepad.

'What? *No*,' said Cora, crinkling her nose.

The fairy crossed off something on his notepad. 'Well, we can safely say you're not a vampire then. They like blood. A lot.'

Cora shuddered.

'You never know,' said Tick with a shrug. 'One minute you're a person. Next minute, vampire. It's very common, you know.'

Cora didn't want to think about how common vampires were. She took a small sip of the soup. It tasted like the tea the fairy godmothers had given her.

'It's myrtle soup,' said Tock. 'An ancient fairy recipe.'

Then there was a *POP!* of magic and Cora found herself no longer wet.

'Thanks,' she said. She quickly finished the soup. She hadn't realised how hungry she was until the myrtle soup hit her stomach.

'While you were asleep, we also crossed off ogre,' said Tock, picking up his notepad.

'And zombie,' added Tock. 'You haven't even tried to eat us once.'

Cora thought the fairy sounded a little offended.

Then with a *POP!* his notepad, pen and glasses disappeared. With another *POP!* so did Tick's.

'There's a gateway not far from here,' Tock said. 'But first,' the fairy stopped and pointed to something

on the cave floor. Cora looked down to find the whisper root next to her. She had almost forgotten about the oddly shaped potato. Carefully, she handed it to the fairy.

Tock held the whisper root into the fire. They watched and waited for something to happen. Then a wisp of thick, black smoke appeared in the flames and gradually more smoke began to fill up the space in the small cave.

Cora screwed up her nose at the smell. It reminded her of the time when Dot had accidentally set the grill too high and burnt their last few pieces of bread. The burnt smell filled up their entire home. Even Scratch refused to go anywhere near the kitchen. When Dot had rescued the bread from the grill, only one of the pieces wasn't badly burnt. And Dot had given it to Cora.

Tock flew over to her with the whisper root in one hand, his other hand holding his nose tightly closed.

Cora stood up.

'Hold still,' Tock said. The fairy waved the whisper root in the air all around her, covering her in the thick, black smoke from the top of her head to the soles of her feet.

Tick watched, pinching his nose closed too and grimacing at the stench.

The smoke swallowed her. All she could see was darkness. Cora closed her eye. Then some of the smoke went up her nose and she coughed and spluttered.

'There,' said Tock after covering her entirely in the whisper root smoke a few times. 'I think that will do.' He blew out the burning embers at the end of the whisper root and handed it back to Cora.

Instead of disappearing into the air, she watched the black smoke that floated around her fall down and settle on top of her skin like a fine layer of dirt. Up close, it gave her pale skin a subtle, grey tint.

'We need to keep moving,' said Tick.

They packed up their things and put out the fire. As they left the cave, Cora thought of Dot. And the dream she had where her arms were made of shadows. She looked down at the glistening smoke that sat on her skin. *Please*, she begged. *Please work.*

Chapter Twenty-Seven

'How far away is the gateway again?' Cora asked. She trudged up the hill behind the flying fairies.

'Not far,' said Tick and Tock at the same time.

Cora was beginning to think the fairies' idea of not far was very different from hers. They had been walking for what felt like a few hours. When they left the cave, Cora was happy to see a landscape of large rolling hills of green with pockets of beautiful trees outside. She had never seen scenery like it. Like The Hollow, she thought it was beautiful. As she walked, she breathed in the air, felt the trees with her hands, and gazed out into the sunny distance. But as the hours passed, her legs had started to hurt. And the air had too many bugs in it. And the sun had become too strong in her eye.

At least, Cora thought, *we are out in the open.* They would be able to see the Jinx from far away. But also, being out in the open, she realised, left them with nowhere to hide. Around her sat trees and grassy hills. They wouldn't do. Perhaps there was another cave somewhere? One that the Jinx wouldn't be able to fit inside?

Cora picked up her pace and caught up to Tick and Tock. 'Where are we?' she asked.

'Somewhere outside Plunk,' said Tick, looking around. 'Archibald probably won't look here first.'

'Probably?' Cora echoed. Her stomach squirmed with unease. She pictured the warlock appearing next to her with a *POP!* at any moment. Then she remembered what happened to Tick and Tock at the witch's shop. What Archibald Drake had done to them. She shuddered at the memory of the fairies sitting suspended in the air, twisting in pain.

'The warlock,' she said. 'Did he … when he … at the witch's shop …?'

Tick and Tock winced.

'It felt like our bones were …' said Tock, trying to find the words.

'… on fire,' finished Tick.

Cora wished she never brought it up.

'If you hadn't have stopped him …' said Tock.

The fairies were silent for a time.

'How did you … *feel* when you faced Archibald at the witch's shop?' asked Tick. 'Had you ever felt like that before?'

Cora thought about the feeling she felt, the one that was with her now all the time, the one that helped her help Tick and Tock in the witch's shop.

'I felt it first at the lake. It's like a feeling under my skin,' she said, trying to explain it. 'Like something that's trying to get out …'

Tick and Tock looked at each other. With a *POP!* both of the fairies had notepads and pens in their hands again. They flew around her as she walked.

'Is it still there?' asked Tock. 'The feeling?'

Cora nodded. Carefully, she felt for it and found it. She had somehow made room for it in the past few days since the lake. Like it was part of her. What that meant, she didn't know.

'The good news is that we can probably cross off troll from the list,' said Tock.

'But you *could* still be a giant,' said Tick. 'Or a witch.'

Cora groaned.

'You have bursts of strength,' said Tock. 'That's what we know.' He scribbled down something on his notepad.

'Do you think you can control it?' Tick asked, peering at her from over his glasses.

Cora wasn't sure. She remembered having the feeling under control until Archibald showed up. 'I'm not sure. Why?'

Tick and Tock stopped flying. They looked at each other.

'We know one thing for sure,' said Tick.

'There's magic inside of you, Cora,' said Tock.

She couldn't help but look down at herself.

'The feeling you describe is not a feeling at all. It's magic,' said Tick.

'Powerful magic,' added Tock. 'It's how you were able to summon the Jinx.'

The fairies tapped their pens on their hairy heads in thought. Then they looked through the notes in their notepads.

'And your bracelet,' said Tock suddenly. 'Maybe …'

'… maybe it *has* been protecting you this whole time,' finished Tick.

Cora looked down at her wrist. She remembered what the witch had said about her bracelet. *Protection from others. Protection from oneself.* It glimmered innocently in the sun.

'It tingles sometimes,' Cora said. 'On my wrist. And it …' she paused, remembering, 'it tingled when I first saw the Jinx and then in The Hollow … and then again in the shop yesterday when Archibald was there.'

Tick and Tock smiled.

'Do you know what this means?' replied Tock excitedly.

Cora hoped it didn't mean she was a giant.

'Now you stand a chance,' said Tick happily.

'At fighting the Jinx,' said Tock, smiling widely.

Cora stopped walking. She looked at the fairies as though they had grown five heads. 'FIGHT the Jinx?!' she cried. 'Are you crazy?!'

'But you fought it already,' said Tock. 'And you survived!'

'Because your bracelet protected you,' said Tick. 'At least we *think* it did.'

'That was … that … I'm not fighting the Jinx,' Cora said. She set off at a brisk walk, away from the fairies.

'Well, of course, not right now,' said Tock, flying after her. 'You're not ready.'

'You need training,' said Tick, flying after her too.

'Training?' Cora asked. 'I'm eleven years old.' She didn't like where this was heading. She didn't like it at all. She was starting to wish she *was* a giant, or a mermaid, or a werewolf.

Tock darted in front of her, stopping Cora in her stride.

'Magic needs to be practised,' he said. 'Otherwise …'

Cora looked at the fairy, uncertain. 'Otherwise?' Otherwise was never good. She did not like otherwise.

'Otherwise,' said Tick, stopping to hover in front of her, too, 'it can turn into something else.'

'Something else?'

'Something uncontrollable,' said Tock.

Cora closed her eye and rubbed her temples.

'The Jinx will be back,' said Tock gently.

'Whether it's in a few days or a few weeks,' said Tick.

'We need to be prepared,' said Tock. 'For Archibald, too.'

Cora swallowed. She pictured herself standing face to face with Archibald and the Jinx. She shook her head.

'Your magic and ours are the best defence we have,' said Tock.

'And the whisper root,' added Tick.

'You can do this,' said Tock. He grabbed her hands.

Cora opened her eye. 'But … I …' she tried. 'I'm just … me.'

Tick and Tock looked at each other, then back at her.

'Not anymore,' said Tick.

Cora took a deep breath. She felt like running away. She felt like going back to Urt and hiding beneath her blanket with Scratch.

'We will help you,' said Tock.

Tick nodded. 'Magic is easy.'

Cora looked from Tick to Tock. If the feeling inside of her *was* magic and she could control it, then maybe it *would* give her enough of a chance. And enough of a chance to find Dot.

Cora squared her shoulders. 'Do you really think I can control it? Whatever this is?'

'There's only one way to find out,' said Tock.

Chapter Twenty-Eight

'I don't know about this,' said Cora.

She stood on a small hill and stretched out before her was a clearing dotted with a handful of stumpy trees. Tick and Tock stood waving to her at the other end of the grassy clearing.

'It will be fish,' Tick called back.

'Fine,' corrected Tock.

'What are you supposed to be, anyway?' she asked.

'I'm a Jinx,' said Tock. He had used magic to dress himself in what looked like a large, black raincoat. He stood up on his tippy toes and spread his arms out wide.

'And I'm a warlock,' Tick said. He was dressed in a black cape that draped over his hairy shoulders.

Cora tried to calm her nerves.

'Just do what you did before,' said Tick.

'But I don't know what I did before,' said Cora. Hesitantly, she found the feeling waiting inside of her.

It was like a calm pool of water she could dip her hand into it. But what was she supposed to do with it? She tried to remember what she had done at The Hollow and then again at the Black Market of Gwell ... but everything had happened so suddenly.

'On the count of three,' called Tock.

'Wait,' said Cora. She wasn't ready.

'Remember to concentrate,' said Tick.

Cora grabbed hold of the feeling. Now what?

Then, quick as a flash, Tock flew up the clearing. Arms raised, he darted full speed towards her and let out a roar.

Cora closed her eye and lifted up her hands in front of her face as he came barrelling at her. She waited. Nothing happened. She opened her eye to find Tock hovering in front of her.

'Anything?' he asked.

Cora shook her head.

Then Tick flew up the clearing, faster than Tock. Cora stood still and tried to focus. She wasn't quite sure what to do with her hands so she held them out in front of her. She tried to push the feeling to the surface. But it stayed still. Tick came to a stop right in front of Cora's outstretched hands. Then with a finger, he poked at her hand.

'Nothing?' he asked.

Cora shook her head.

Tock flew at her again, this time sending *POP!s* of magic at her. Cora ducked and jumped out of the way of the sparks. But she was so busy avoiding them that she completely forgot about holding onto the feeling inside of her. By the time Tock reached her, she was bent over with her hands on her knees, out of breath.

Cora sighed. She felt like she was failing more of Dot's drills.

'Perhaps we should try another day,' offered Tick.

Cora shook her head. With Archibald and the Jinx on their tail, they didn't have days to waste. Tock was right. Whatever she had, she needed to know how to control it. She had to keep trying. Cora squared her shoulders. 'Again.'

Tick and Tock flew towards her at the same time. Then with a *POP!* of magic, Tock disappeared. Cora waited, hands out. She looked to her left and her right. Then the fairy suddenly reappeared next to her. 'Boo!' he cried.

Cora shrieked and jumped in the air. But, still, no magic. 'Again,' she puffed.

Tick and Tock once again flew towards her. This time from two different sides of the clearing. Then they both disappeared and reappeared behind her. Cora twisted around, tripped over her feet and fell to

the ground. With a groan, she stood up and dusted herself off. 'Again,' she said.

They continued like this for an hour. Each time Tick and Tock tried something different but each time, Cora wasn't able to summon her magic.

When they eventually stopped, the three of them sat on the hill, exhausted. Defeated, Cora looked down at her hands. She imagined herself standing in front of the Jinx and the warlock trying to summon her magic, failing and being eaten or worse, suspended in the air in pain like Tick and Tock had been.

'I don't think I can do this,' Cora whispered.

Tick and Tock looked over at her.

'There has to be something we're missing,' said Tick.

Like what? thought Cora. They had tried everything. Would the magic only appear when she didn't want it to? Then a glimmer caught her eye. *Her bracelet.* She realised that it hadn't tingled once on her wrist.

'A lot of magic is connected to emotions,' said Tock, scratching his chin in thought.

'Try summoning the feelings you had at the lake,' said Tick.

Cora thought back. *Focus*, she said to herself. It wasn't difficult to remember how she felt. 'I … I couldn't breathe,' she said. 'The Jinx was squeezing me tight.' She paused and waited for something to happen. The calm pool of water moved beneath her skin.

'Wait,' she gasped. And then as quickly as it started, it stopped. Cora let out a cry of frustration.

'I … I'm sorry,' she said, giving up. Because of her they no longer stood a chance against the Jinx or the warlock. She no longer had a chance of seeing Dot again.

Tick and Tock said something to her but Cora couldn't make out what it was. She looked over at them but their voices sounded far away. Then Tick and Tock started to look blurry. She closed her eye and opened it again. But the fairies were still fuzzy and their voices were like echoes in her ears.

Suddenly, a crack of pain shot through Cora's head.

'Argh!' she cried out.

The sharp pain flew through her body. The pain ripped through her like an earthquake. She threw her hands to the ground. She felt the earth beneath her start to rumble and shake.

Something had taken a hold of her. What was

once a calm pool of water was now an out-of-control ocean in her mind. She couldn't stop it. She couldn't even hold onto it. There was too much to hold onto. It swept over her in gallons and gallons of waves.

'Cora!' the fairies cried.

She closed her eye and held her hands to her head. She let out another cry of pain but it didn't sound like her. It sounded like a ... like a roar. She couldn't take it anymore. She felt like something was going to burst out of her skin.

'Make it stop,' she breathed. 'Please.'

'It's your magic!' said Tick.

'Put it away!' yelled Tock.

Cora heard the fairy's voice clearly this time. *Put it away? How?* She opened her eye to find the fairies kneeling in front of her, eyes wide.

'Think of a box or a jar or something to put it in!' cried Tick.

Cora couldn't think. The pounding in her ears and the pain was too much. She felt her bracelet tingle. Then she thought of Dot. And her bookcase that sat in their home in Urt. She knew it like the back of her hand. Cora pictured it and grabbed a book on the top shelf. She opened it and shoved the pain inside it. Then, snapping the cover shut, she put it back on the bookcase.

And just like that, the pain stopped. The calm pool of water returned. And Cora felt like herself again. She laid back on the grass, breathing heavily.

Tick and Tock looked around them.

'I think that's enough practice for today,' said Tock.

Chapter Twenty-Nine

Cora trudged along behind the fairies in silence. She replayed what had happened over and over in her head. *What was that?!* She tried to remember what she had done. The strange pain she had felt still lingered on the edges. As she walked, she decided that the feeling she had, the magic, whatever it was, she didn't want it. She didn't want any of it.

Tick and Tock turned around to face her as they flew backwards.

'Well, I think we can say that your first attempt at using magic was a success,' said Tick with a smile.

There was a pause. Cora looked up at them. 'A success?!' she echoed. Had they lost their minds? How was any part of what had happened a success?

Tick and Tock nodded.

'We think the magic was trying to control you,' said Tick.

'And you didn't let it,' said Tock.

'So it was a success!' said Tick.

'Really?' Cora queried.

Tick and Tock nodded.

'Every magic is different,' said Tock. 'Just like every person.'

'And we still have a lot of magical beings on our list to cross off,' added Tick. There was a *POP!* of magic and the fairy held his notepad in his hand again.

'We can cross off centaur,' said Tock.

'Maybe not just yet,' said Tick with a smile.

Cora groaned. She knew what the fairies were doing. They were trying to make her feel better. But it just made her feel worse. She shook her head at them. 'I can't do this,' she said.

'Do what?' asked Tock.

'This,' said Cora coming to a stop. 'Be magic.' She looked down at her feet. She felt a tear reach her eye. One thing was for certain — the magic inside of her scared her now more than ever. She wished she could just go back to the way things were when she was in Urt. When she was with Dot. 'I just … want to go home.'

The fairies flew down by her side.

'It will get easier,' said Tick gently.

'You've already done the hardest part,' said Tock.

'And practice makes purple,' said Tick.

Cora paused. 'Perfect,' she corrected.

'Really?' replied Tick. 'Not purple?'

Cora shook her head but couldn't help the small smile that reached her lips. She swiped at her eye.

'What if it happens again?' she asked. 'What if I can't control it the next time?' And what if she did something worse … what if next time she hurt Tick or Tock? Or someone else she cared about?

Tick and Tock looked down.

Then Tock looked up suddenly. 'You will,' he said confidently.

'She will?' asked Tick, doubtfully.

Tock elbowed Tick in the ribs. 'You will because we know someone who can help.'

'You do?' Cora replied.

'Yeah, we do?' asked Tick, rubbing his ribs.

'At least … I hope she can,' said Tock.

Cora wasn't so sure. The last time the fairies knew someone who could help, she had ended up destroying their entire kingdom and getting them banished. She hoped the whisper root was enough to keep the Jinx away. At least for a little while longer.

'The gateway is close,' said Tick, flying ahead of them.

The fairies flew up the hill and Cora walked up the steep, grassy slope. When she got to the top, she noticed that sitting below them, alone in a field, was a small, wooden cabin.

Tick pointed down towards it. 'There,' he said.

The fairies flew down the hill and Cora followed on foot. When they reached the cabin, the fairies knocked on the door.

The door opened and a man stood behind it. He had long hair tied back into a knot, no eyebrows and one of his pant legs ended at his knee. When he saw Tick and Tock, he stuck out his bare leg and put his hands on his hips.

'What do you think?' he asked.

'Hello Earl,' said Tock. 'Did the wood nymph steal your pant leg again?'

Earl nodded before turning and walking back inside the cabin, leaving the door open.

Tick, Tock and Cora followed him.

'Third time this week,' said Earl.

The inside of the cabin was compact and uncluttered. A chair stood in the middle of the room and a small table sat nearby. On the far wall were three clocks. Each of them showed a different time and the hands on them moved backwards at different speeds. The man walked up to the chair in the middle of the room and pushed it to the side. Then he bent down and with a piece of chalk he drew a triangle on the wooden floor. The lines glowed blue, then the floor inside the triangle disappeared and a swirl of blue light sat in its place.

When the man stood up, he looked over at Cora. 'I've got one of those,' he said proudly. Then he rolled up one of his shirtsleeves to reveal a scar across one of his arms. Cora noticed that his scar was flat and white instead of bumpy and red like hers.

'Did you hear?' Earl asked the fairies. 'About the Jinx that's on the loose?'

Cora looked at Tick and Tock.

'Where?' replied Tock worriedly.

'It was spotted not far from here. Over in Berry Nest.'

'That's not far at all,' said Tick to Cora.

Cora's heart quickened. She was running out of time.'We must hurry,' said Tock. 'To the Oak Wood.'

Tick and Tock jumped into the swirling blue gateway. Cora didn't want to be left behind. She gave a wave goodbye to the man with the missing pant leg and jumped in after the fairies, diving into the swirling blue light.

Chapter Thirty

There was a loud sucking noise, followed by a *POP!* and Cora found herself flying through the air and then landing with a *SPLOSH* … right into a flowing stream. She sat up with a gasp as the cold water soaked every inch of her. Then she stood up and trampled out of the stream onto the rocks nearby. She looked around to find Tick and Tock fluttering their wings from a safe distance away, smiles on their faces.

Cora flicked her wet hair out of her face. 'Really?'

'The gateway is not an exact science,' said Tock apologetically.

Then there was a *POP!* and Cora was dry again.

'Thank you,' she said. She looked around them. 'Where are we?' The stream she had fallen into ran through a wood. She could see a squat house sitting up ahead.

'The Oak Wood,' said Tock.

'We know someone who lives here,' said Tick. 'Or we *did* know someone who lives here.'

'Someone who might be able to help you with your magic,' said Tock.

'Are you sure she wants to see us?' Tick asked Tock. 'Last time …'

'Last time was an accident,' said Tock. 'Besides, last time was also a long time ago. Belle would have forgotten.'

Cora and the fairies followed the stream up into the wood. When they got to the house that sat at the top, they stopped.

Cora saw that it wasn't a normal-sized house. It was much smaller and much rounder than any house she had ever seen. She would have to crouch to fit inside the small, orange door.

'What are you two doing here?' came a voice from behind them.

Cora turned around to see a woman carrying a basket of vegetables. She was shorter than Cora and her skin was a light shade of green. Her dark hair fell in plaits by her pointed ears.

Before they could answer, the woman reached into her basket, picked up an onion and threw it at them! It tore past them, just missing Tock's head. Then suddenly one after another, she threw more vegetables

at them. Cabbages! Turnips! Lettuces! Sweet potatoes! Everything and anything the woman could get her hands on was flung straight at Tick and Tock.

'Looks like she hasn't forgotten,' said Cora with a smile, as she dodged a flying radish.

When the woman ran out of vegetables in her basket, Cora heard the tinkling of a bell and then the woman's basket was full again.

Uh-oh.

The woman threw a beetroot at them and then another whole lettuce head. The fairies tried to dodge the flying vegetables that were flung their way.

'Belle! Belle! It's us! Tick and Tock!' said Tock, his hands raised innocently in the air.

'I know!' said Belle. She threw some tomatoes and then a cauliflower.

Tick and Tock ducked and dived but it was impossible to avoid being hit. The woman had very accurate aim.

When the woman's basket became empty again, she stopped. She glared at the fairies as she huffed and puffed. Tock was covered in cabbage leaves and Tick was dripping in drooping spinach pieces.

'Why are you here?' Belle asked.

'We need your help,' said Tick.

'A very angry Archibald Drake along with a very angry Jinx are not far behind us,' said Tock.

'Why would I help you? After what you did,' said Belle.

Tick looked at Tock.

'We're sorry,' said Tock. 'It was an accident. Honest.'

'A lot has changed since you last saw us,' said Tick.

'Leave,' Belle said.

'We didn't mean to tell them where you were,' said Tick.

'It just … slipped out,' said Tock.

Cora could see that Tick and Tock weren't getting anywhere. The woman still looked very angry. 'Let's just go,' said Cora.

Tick and Tock turned to her.

'Belle is a goblin,' whispered Tock.

'Hobgoblin,' the woman corrected, clearly listening.

'She knows a lot about magic,' said Tick.

'More than these two,' said the woman.

'She could help you,' said Tock.

Cora looked over at the small, green woman. Perhaps she could try to persuade her?

'Please,' said Cora. 'You wouldn't be helping them. You would be helping me.'

The woman looked at Cora and crossed her arms. 'Who are you?'

Cora thought for a minute. 'I'm the reason why there is a very angry warlock and a very angry Jinx not far behind us,' she said. 'I have some kind of magic and I have no idea how to use it.'

The small, green woman looked at her with interest. Her eyes moved to where Cora's eye used to be and then to where Cora's bracelet sat on her wrist.

The woman paused. Then she stalked towards them, glaring at Tick and Tock. She pushed past them still glaring at Tick and Tock and entered her house.

Even though Belle was inside her house, Cora could still feel the hobgoblin's stare. Tick, Tock and Cora stood where they were, uncertain.

'Let's go,' said Tick.

'Wait a moment,' said Tock, listening for something.

Then from inside the house, Belle called out to them. 'Come in. But don't touch anything.'

Chapter Thirty-One

*C*ora crouched down as she entered the hobgoblin's house. The inside was bigger than Cora had expected and she was relieved to find that she could stand up. Green vines from potted plants hung down from the ceiling and in the centre of the room stood a comfortable chair in front of a fireplace. A small fire crackled there.

Cora was about to ask if she needed to take off her shoes but when she looked down she found that she wasn't stepping on a wooden or concrete floor. Instead, beneath her feet was an earthen floor.

'Sit,' said the hobgoblin as she pulled out a chair near a table made from gnarled tree branches.

Cora sat down obediently. Near her, on top of the table, were three bowls. One was filled with freshly plucked feathers, another with dark stones and the third was filled with what looked like white chalk dust.

Belle pulled out another chair and sat down in front of Cora. From close up, Cora noticed the woman wore a necklace that had a piece of wood carved into the letter 'S' hanging from it.

'It's charmed,' said the hobgoblin, noticing her gaze. 'Just like your bracelet.'

Cora stopped. She looked down at her wrist. 'How did you know it's charmed?'

The hobgoblin held up her hand, brushing away the question. 'What did you do to annoy a warlock and a Jinx?' she asked, fixing her with a stern gaze.

There was something about the woman's green, unblinking stare that made Cora feel uneasy. She looked over at Tick and Tock who stood watching nearby. The fairies nodded.

'I threw the warlock through a window and hit the Jinx across a lake,' said Cora slowly.

The woman sat back in her chair. 'Really?'

Cora nodded and looked away.

'I'm impressed,' said Belle with a small smile.

'So were we,' said Tick.

Cora didn't feel very impressive. She felt very far from impressive.

'The Jinx curse is too powerful. Almost impossible to break,' said Belle, shaking her head.

'We know,' said Tick, Tock and Cora at the same time.

'Cora's magic ... it's not like any we've ever seen,' said Tick.

The hobgoblin squinted at the fairies. 'How so?'

'It's ... strong and ... unpredictable,' said Tock.

'Possibly ... uncontrollable,' added Tick, looking away.

Belle turned back to Cora. 'What does it feel like?' she asked.

Cora tried to put the feeling into words. 'It feels like ... water. Like a pool of water, just sitting there, inside,' she said. 'And when I tried to use it ...'

'It wouldn't let you,' finished the hobgoblin.

Cora nodded.

The hobgoblin sat in thought for a moment until she said, 'It wants to be used. Magic always does. But you must let it become part of you. Don't resist it.'

Cora wasn't sure she wanted it to be part of her. The thought of it made her squirm with dread.

'Only when it is part of you, can you control it,' said the hobgoblin. 'Otherwise ...'

There was that word again. *Otherwise.*

'You said it is like a pool of water?' Belle asked.

Cora nodded.

'Well,' said Belle, clapping her hands together, 'you must empty it.'

Cora stared back at the woman. 'Empty it?' she asked. *That was it?* Cora thought. *That was all it took?* She looked over at Tick and Tock. They shrugged.

The hobgoblin nodded.

'How?' Cora asked.

'Close your eyes … I mean *eye* …' said Belle.

Cora closed her eye.

'Find the pool of water,' came Belle's voice.

Cora found it.

'And just let the water leave,' Belle said.

That was the hard part. Cora tried to let it leave. At least she *thought* she did. But the pool of water didn't go anywhere. She gave it a small push. Yet it stayed right where it was. She took a deep breath. *Focus*, she said to herself. She imagined the water disappearing. She imagined it flowing down a drain. Then she took another look at it and noticed that the pool had become smaller. It was shrinking! Until, eventually, it was gone.

When she opened her eye, Tick's and Tock's eager faces greeted her.

'Did it work?' they asked at the same time.

'I … I don't know,' she said honestly. The pool of

water was gone but she didn't feel any different. She felt the same.

'Stand up and let's have a look at what you can do,' said Belle.

Cora stood up carefully from her seat. She wasn't sure what to do. Without the pool of water, there was nothing for her to grab onto or to push aside or lock away. She closed her eye. She waited for the magic to appear. Then she felt it. Something small like a butterfly, fluttered within her. She tried to catch it but as soon as she felt it, it disappeared.

Cora shook her head. 'I think I might be broken,' she said.

Belle let out a small laugh. She stood up and handed her the chair she had been sitting on. 'The magic is now part of you.'

Cora held the wooden chair in her hands, confused.

'Break it,' said the hobgoblin.

Cora looked down at the chair. It was made out of thick tree branches that were woven into shape. There was no way she would be able to break it. She closed her eye. The butterfly was back. She concentrated and then pulled the chair with both of her hands … and with a *CRACK!* it completely shattered into two parts!

Cora stared wide-eyed at the pieces of chair in her hands.

Tick and Tock clapped happily.

Belle smiled. 'It will take some practice, turning it on and off,' she said. 'Now open that door.' Belle pointed to a door that sat wedged into the tree wall.

Cora walked over to it and, grabbing it by the handle, she pulled … and with a groan the entire door flew out from the wall!

Tick, Tock and Belle ducked as the door went flying past them.

'Oops,' Cora said. A fear settled inside her as she stared at the door. *How did I do that?*

'That,' Belle said, 'was my favourite door.'

'What! Oh, I'm sorry,' said Cora. She picked it up and tried to put the door back in its place on the wall.

Belle laughed. 'I'm only kidding.'

'Wait until Archibald sees what you can do!' said Tick with a clap of his hands.

Belle stopped laughing. 'Archibald?' she echoed, her smile fading faster than a dropped stone. 'Archibald Drake? The warlock?'

Chapter Thirty-Two

Tick and Tock nodded at Belle.

'Explain,' Belle said seriously. 'Now.' The hobgoblin stared at the fairies. 'You haven't played one of your tricks on him, have you?'

'No!' said Tick adamantly.

'He's been after us ever since we delivered a message to him,' said Tock.

'What message?' Belle asked. Cora could see something flicker in Belle's eyes. *Fear.*

Tick shrugged. 'Father gave it to us,' he said.

Cora stared at the fairies. *Father?* she thought.

'That was ... before he banished us,' said Tock.

Cora almost gasped. *King Clang was Tick and Tock's father?!* She looked over at the fairies. Why hadn't they told her? Then she realised that King Clang had banished his own sons ... because of her. The soup in her stomach suddenly sloshed around uncomfortably.

'What does Drake want?' Belle asked.

Tick and Tock looked at Cora. The hobgoblin moved her eyes to her too, and there was a silence around the table.

'You're not from this world, are you?' Belle asked.

Cora shook her head. 'I don't know what world I'm from,' she mumbled truthfully.

'You're one of us,' the hobgoblin said. 'Anyone can sense it. Even them.' She looked over at Tick and Tock. 'But what kind … I don't know.' She tilted her head at Cora.

Cora sighed.

'You're not a witch,' said the hobgoblin.

Cora looked over at Tick and Tock as if to say, *I told you so.*

'It takes years for witches to be able to master breaking apart a chair without at least muttering a spell. No, you're much more … advanced,' she said.

Cora frowned. That didn't sound good.

'And you've been marked,' she said, pointing a finger towards Cora's bumpy, red scar.

'I … that's just …' said Cora.

The woman nodded. 'Witches leave marks like that.'

Tick and Tock looked at her as if to say, *we told you so.*

Cora remembered what Tick and Tock had called it. *The witch's mark.* But to her, it was just … her. Then she remembered the jar of troll eyes in the witch's shop. Was there a witch somewhere out there who had her eye in a jar? She shuddered at the thought.

Then Cora asked something she had been wondering for a while. 'If I'm not a witch … then what am I?' she asked.

'Give me your hands,' said Belle. Her unsettling green stare returned.

Cora looked at Tick and Tock, unsure. They shrugged.

Hesitantly, she held out her hands across the table towards the hobgoblin. Belle grabbed them tightly in her green ones and closed her eyes.

Cora did the same. She felt a strange feeling go through her, like a spark of electricity. Then it felt like someone was looking inside her, searching for something. Suddenly, the hobgoblin let go of her hands.

Cora opened her eye.

Belle quickly stood up from her seat. 'You're um …' she said, stepping away from the table. 'Not like … anything I've ever seen.' She walked to the fireplace and pulled out a kettle from a cupboard beside it. She hung it over the fire.

'But you've lived for a thousand years,' said Tock.

'You've seen everything,' said Tick.

Belle didn't answer them. Instead she busied herself with making a pot of tea.

'Are you alright, Belle?' Tock asked.

'Yes, yes, would anyone like a cup of tea?' she asked, not looking up from the fire.

Tick and Tock looked at each other.

'What did you see?' Cora asked. She stood up from the table. There was something about the way the hobgoblin was acting that worried her. She was different. Cora's stomach squirmed with uneasiness.

The hobgoblin looked over at her. Her green eyes flickered with fear again.

'I saw …' she said with a shake of her head. 'Something not possible.'

Cora looked over at the fairies.

'Not possible?' asked Tock.

Now Cora really felt sick. She walked over towards the hobgoblin. 'Please,' she said.

The hobgoblin looked at her. 'I saw …' she said in a whisper that only Cora could hear. 'I saw a Jinx.'

A Jinx?! Cora felt like she was going to faint. Her dream, the one with Dot, suddenly came rushing to her mind. The one where she had shadows for arms. A Jinx.

Cora took a step backwards. Her mind was suddenly flooded with images of herself as a shadow creature. How would it happen? Would she wake up one morning huge and shadowy? How long did she have?

The hobgoblin paused. 'No,' she said. 'You can't!' Cora looked around. Who was she talking to?

Then Belle grabbed onto her necklace. It glowed a bright yellow.

She looked up at the fairies, eyes wide. 'Run,' she whispered.

Then the hobgoblin smiled an unusual smile. Like she was being forced by someone they couldn't see. Then Belle let out a soft, deep laugh that wasn't her own.

'Belle?' said Tick.

'Not anymore,' the hobgoblin said. Then she held up her hands and Tick went flying into a wall.

'The hobgoblin was strong,' said Belle. 'But not strong enough.'

'No!' said Tock. He flew up from his seat and darted towards Belle.

But she fell to the ground. Cora stared down at her, wide-eyed. Next to her, the air shimmered.

Cora's bracelet tingled on her wrist. *Oh no.*

Tick and Tock stopped in mid-air. Standing in the hobgoblin's home was none other than the powerful warlock, Archibald Drake.

Chapter Thirty-Three

*C*ora now stared wide-eyed at the warlock in front of her. When Archibald Drake's eyes met hers, he smiled.

'Go!' cried Tock.

Cora watched as the warlock held his hands up and suddenly the walls of the hobgoblin's home started to shake. Then the objects around them lifted up and one by one, they hurtled through the air towards Cora. Pots, pans, cushions, clocks. Everything in the house headed straight for her.

Cora froze in place. She didn't know what to do. She looked around and grabbed the door that she had pulled off the wall from the floor and held it in front of her like a shield. The objects hit the door and ricocheted off.

BANG! CLUNK! CLANK! CLINK!

Peering over the door, Cora watched as Tick and Tock threw *POP!s* of magic at the warlock. Archibald ducked and wove and held his hand up as magic sparks went whizzing past him.

Then, remembering her magic, Cora threw the door she held in her hands at the warlock. It shot towards him with lightning speed, but right at the last minute Archibald pushed the door aside with his magic, embedding it into the wall next to him.

'Impressive,' the warlock said.

Tick and Tock sped over to Cora, grasped her shoulder and then with a *POP!* they were gone from the hobgoblin's home.

Cora blinked and found herself outside near a waterfall. She held her hands up to her ears against the loud roar of the water. Tick and Tock hovered in the air next to her, their eyes wide with panic.

Tick twirled around to face Tock. 'How did Drake —'

'Possession,' said Tock.

Tick's eyes widened.

'Dark magic,' said Tick to Cora. 'Used to control other magical beings.'

'It's forbidden. Even for warlocks,' said Tock.

'Is Belle alright?' Cora asked worriedly.

Tock nodded. 'She will be. Once she regains her strength.'

The fairies paused. They looked to their left and in front of them, the air shimmered.

'Uh-oh,' said Tick.

The shimmer turned into a shape and in seconds, Archibald Drake was standing in front of them again, a smile on his face.

Crud.

Tock threw a *POP!* of magic at the warlock and then he and Tick grabbed Cora. With another *POP!* they were gone from the waterfall.

Cora found herself standing in the middle of a small road. It was almost dark.

Tick and Tock were bent over, out of breath. They shook their heads, unable to speak.

Then Cora saw the air behind the fairies shimmer slightly. She pointed, eyes wide. 'Guys,' she said warningly.

Tick and Tock turned around to see Archibald Drake shimmer into place again. The fairies dove towards Cora, touched her and with a *POP!* they were somewhere else.

'Take her,' said Tick urgently. 'I'll lead him away,'

'No,' said Tock.

'He's tracing our magic,' said Tick. 'I'll meet you at the gateway in Jade City. Go!'

And then with a *POP!* Tick was gone.

'Tick!' said Tock.

But before they could do anything, a shimmer started to appear in the air near them. Tock seized Cora and magicked them both away.

In a blink, Cora and Tock were in an alleyway. It was well and truly dark now. They waited, holding their breath. Cora whirled around on the spot, trying to see a shimmer in the air that was bound to come. Minutes went by and no shimmer appeared.

Cora let out an uneasy breath.

'I should have known something was wrong!' said Tock. The fairy kicked over a bucket that sat on the ground nearby. 'Belle tried to warn us.'

The hobgoblin had helped her with her magic. Cora shuddered at the thought of what the warlock could have done if he had captured them. Then she thought of Tick. He had risked himself so that she could get away.

Tock sat on the ground, his head bent low in defeat. Cora walked over and sat down next to him.

'I hope Tick is alright,' she said.

'I hope so, too,' said Tock.

They sat in silence for a moment.

'I'm sorry, Cora,' said Tock.

Cora looked at Tock's worried face. 'It's okay,' she said. She put a hand on the fairy's arm. 'Tick will be back.'

Tock gave her a small, unsure smile.

Then Cora remembered what the hobgoblin had told her. She had seen *a Jinx* inside of her. Cora swallowed and pushed the thought aside. 'We should keep moving.'

Tock nodded.

Cora walked down the alleyway as Tock flew by her side. When they came to the end of it, Cora looked out to see a city lit up spectacularly in the night. Jade City.

'Wow,' Cora muttered.

It was a sea of colour. Small houses with pointed gold spires and tall buildings with glass domes were glowing in hues of purple and pink. Even the pristine cobblestones beneath her feet were painted in soft, shimmering colours. She had never seen anything like it. She could hear distant *POP!s* of magic in the air and there was music coming from somewhere not far away.

'Magical beings from all over come to Jade City,' said Tock.

Cora looked up and around as they walked. She noticed tiny, sparkling creatures zipping about in the air above them. Then Cora almost bumped into a tall woman wearing a sparkling red dress and walking in her direction. In one of her hands, the woman carried a matching red umbrella that shone in the light.

'Sorry,' Cora said, stepping out of the way. The woman glanced down at her before moving off and as she walked by, Cora noticed that she had four feet and that they made a *CLOMP CLOMP* sound as she walked.

'Centaur,' whispered Tock.

They continued through the city and soon came to a bridge that crossed over a small canal. Cora wasn't surprised to see the water beneath it sparkle a bright, shimmering blue.

A man with two large antlers sat on the edge of the canal, his feet dangling in the water. He waved up at them and Cora waved back. Jade City was nothing like Urt.

'The gateway is not far from here,' said Tock. 'We should stay near it in case Tick … we should stay near it.'

Cora nodded.

When they were closer to the centre of the city, Tock stopped outside a small, red building. Across the top it read, in glowing green letters, GATEWAY. It wasn't hidden like the others they had found.

A woman floated by them on the street. Cora stopped. She could see right through her. Then the woman turned and floated towards the red building and straight through the wall.

'This way,' said Tock.

The fairy flew past the entrance to the gateway building. A few buildings down, he turned left. At the back of a round yellow building, Tock stopped outside a round metal door that stuck out from the ground.

The fairy pulled on the metal door handle with his fairy arms but it remained firmly shut.

Cora looked down at her hands. *Practice makes purple*, she remembered Tick's words.

'Let me try,' she said. Then she took a deep breath and put both hands on the door handle. Cora pulled gently and the metal door swung open.

Inside was a staircase that led into a cramped, dark room. There were used candles resting on upturned boxes and crates. A small pile of blankets lay on the cement floor.

'Have you stayed here before?' Cora asked.

Tock nodded.

They lay down and waited. Cora heard the light drumming of rain on the roof.

Minutes and then soon hours passed. The evening stretched into night. And there was still no sign of Tick. Cora looked over at Tock's worried face.

Any minute now, thought Cora. She waited and waited. Eventually Cora found herself dozing off, her worried thoughts on nothing else but Tick.

Chapter Thirty-Four

There was a fluttering noise in Cora's ear. She turned around and opened her eye to find the tiny room bathed in morning sun. She also found Tock, flying frantically around in the air.

Cora remembered where she was and sat up quickly. She looked around. And her heart fell. There was still no Tick.

'He should have been here by now,' said Tock. He had his hands behind his back as he flew back and forth in the little room.

Cora wondered if the fairy had slept at all.

'Maybe he lost track of time,' Cora said, trying to think of a reason for why Tick wasn't back yet. A reason other than being chased by a powerful and mad warlock.

Tock shook his head. 'Something's happened,' he said, his face grim. 'Something bad.'

Guilt ate at Cora. Why had she let Tick go? She should have stopped Archibald as soon as she saw him in the hobgoblin's home. She should have done something, anything! Why had she just done nothing? Then Tick could have been safe. She thought about everything the fairies had done for her.

Then on the other side of the room, there was a loud *POP!* of magic.

Tock and Cora spun around towards it.

Tick hovered in the air at the back of the room.

'Tick!' they cried.

But Tick didn't respond. He staggered in the air as he flew towards them. His eyes were barely open. Then he fell. Tock flew to him and caught him before he could hit the ground.

'Tick!' Tock exclaimed fearfully.

Cora could see that one of Tick's wings wasn't fluttering like it was supposed to. The wing was bent oddly and the top of it where it was supposed to be transparent was charred black.

'Lay him down,' Cora said. She jumped to her feet and pushed together the blankets to make a bed on the floor.

Tock placed his brother gently down on them.

Cora could hear that Tick's breathing was strained and heavy. And as she looked down at him, she noticed a large red gash on his dainty right arm. Cora swallowed.

'Is he going to be okay?' Cora asked.

'I don't know,' said Tock. He sat by his brother's side. And he and Cora waited. She felt like it was the longest time she had waited for anything.

Hours passed and Cora looked over at Tock. His face was pale.

'I'll be back,' the fairy said.

'Where are you —'

But before she could finish her question, there was a *POP!* of magic and Tock was gone.

The room was silent. It was filled only by Tick's strained breathing. Cora looked over at the fairy. Then she grabbed her pack. She rummaged through it and found the scarf Dot had packed for her. She paused, feeling its woollen threads beneath her fingers. Then Cora pulled each end, ripping it in half.

Carefully, she wrapped a piece of the torn scarf around Tick's injured arm. The fairy murmured in his sleep. What had Archibald done to him? She pictured the warlock hurting her friend and felt like ripping something else in half.

There was a *POP!* and Cora turned to find Tock. He carried in his hands three big bowls of steaming myrtle soup, a bottle of what looked like mud, a loaf of bread and a bag of purple lollies.

'Plum drops,' said Tock with a shrug. 'They're his favourite.'

Tock placed the items on the floor. Then opening the bottle of mud, he carefully spread a thick layer of it over Tick's wounds. 'Honeysuckle paste. It should help.'

Cora and Tock watched and waited.

When the mud on Tick's wounds had completely dried and the morning sun was replaced by the afternoon, Tick opened an eye.

'Are you alright?' Cora asked.

Tick nodded.

'What happened?' asked Tock gently. 'Archibald, did he … is he …?'

'Lost him,' Tick croaked. 'I think.' He sat up, grimacing in pain.

Tock handed him a bowl of myrtle soup and he ate it happily. Cora and Tock ate their myrtle soup too, watching Tick worriedly.

When the fairy finished, he spotted the bag of purple lollies.

'Are those plum drops?' he asked from his place on the blankets. Cora noticed that Tick's eyes were brighter than they were before as they focused intently on the bag of plum drops.

Tick smiled as Tock handed him the bag.

'What happened?' Cora asked between mouthfuls of soup.

'The warlock chased me all the way to Trufford Lake,' said Tick.

Tock stopped slurping. 'Troll Town?!'

Tick nodded.

Cora didn't know where Trufford Lake or Troll Town were but by the surprised look on Tock's face, she assumed they were very far.

'Then,' continued Tick, 'when he realised Cora wasn't with me, he … well … you know.' Tick held up his hands and scrunched his face into a snarl, impersonating the warlock using magic.

'Your wing,' said Cora.

Tick nodded. 'I got away just in time.' He looked over his shoulder at his injured wing sadly. He tried to flutter it but it flapped slowly. Tick winced in pain.

'We need to get it fixed,' said Tock, finishing his soup.

'How?' asked Cora. Every time she had a scrape or a cut, Dot was always the one who mended it. She remembered the little case Dot would take out to bandage her up.

'He needs a fairy healer,' said Tock. 'We have to go to the Fairy Fountain.'

Tick shook his head. 'We're banished, Tock. If they recognise us …'

'The Fairy Fountain?' Cora asked.

'It's where fairies go when they come to Jade City,' said Tock.

'We can't,' said Tick. 'Look, I'm fine,' he tried to fly up into the air but fell crashing down onto the blankets.

Cora turned to Tock. She had made up her mind. 'Can they fix Tick?' she asked.

Tock nodded.

'Then I guess it's settled,' said Cora. 'To the Fairy Fountain.'

Chapter Thirty-Five

Tick, Tock and Cora left the small room and walked out into the bright afternoon sun. The brilliant colours of Jade City were even brighter in the middle of the day. Magical beings of all kinds filled the colourful streets. Some had wings, some had scales, some glided and some stomped. Some even appeared in the middle of the street in a flurry of flames or a puff of smoke.

Tick walked by Cora's side while Tock flew ahead of them, leading the way. Across the road, a pair of trolls yelled at each other.

'Did you do this?' Tick asked Cora, holding up the arm that had half of a scarf wrapped around the top of it.

Cora nodded.

'Thank you,' said Tick. 'It's very nice.'

'Dot made it for me,' Cora said. She was glad she could use the scarf to help her friend. Dot wouldn't have minded.

They weaved their way through Jade City until the three of them eventually came to a stop outside a miniature brown door. Across the top of the door were markings Cora couldn't understand.

Tock knocked three times on the door. Then a tiny window in the middle of the wooden door slid open. Two beady brown eyes stared back at them.

'Yes?' the voice grumbled.

'Three, please,' said Tock.

The two beady eyes looked at Cora questioningly.

'Three?' he asked.

Tock nodded.

'It's three gold coins if you want to enter,' said the fairy behind the door.

'What?' replied Tick. 'Since when?'

'Since a creature destroyed The Hollow,' said the fairy.

'Please,' said Tock, 'my brother is injured.'

'Three gold coins and I will ignore that she's not a fairy.'

Tick and Tock looked at Cora. Tock shrugged.

Cora wasn't taking no for an answer. Tick needed help. But she didn't have any coins. All she had was …

'Shoe polish,' she said.

'Huh?' responded the fairy behind the door.

'Shoe polish,' Cora said again. She dove into her pack and pulled out the round container. Dot had said it would be useful. She looked it over with her eye. It was the last thing she had ever collected in Urt. It seemed so long ago when she had found it. So much had happened. It reminded her of Dot.

'This,' she said holding it up, 'is worth at least three packets of porridge … I mean, three gold coins.'

The fairy stuck his hairy hand through the opening in the door.

Cora shook her head, remembering what had happened in Urt the first time she had found shoe polish.

The fairy grumbled something and slid the window shut.

Please, please, Cora begged in her mind. She hoped it would work.

The door swung open. Cora smiled. The fairy stood by the open door, his palm out. She handed the shoe polish to him and tried to ignore the feeling that she was giving away a part of herself.

When the three of them entered the Fairy Fountain, Cora was surprised to see that behind the door was a smaller version of The Hollow. The trees, the lights, the music and even the small, round huts sat around a tiny pond in front of her.

As they looked around, some fairies flew about and some lounged in chairs. Cora looked over at Tick and Tock. They had smiles on their faces. She wondered if Tick and Tock missed The Hollow like she missed Dot.

'You both have a lot of nerve showing up here,' said a voice from behind them.

Tick, Tock and Cora turned around to find three fairies standing behind them. Two had their hands on their hips and one fairy with hair tangled into two long plaits on either side of his head, pointed a finger at Tick and Tock.

'The Fairy Fountain is open to everyone,' said Tock.

'Including smelly fairies like you, Glug,' added Tick with a smile.

'We know what happened at The Hollow,' said Glug, the fairy with the plaits.

'You're not even allowed to be here,' said another fairy with hair cascading down from his ears to his knees.

Cora remembered what Tick had said. Being banished from The Hollow also meant being banished from the Fairy Fountain.

'I don't think you heard correctly, Thump,' said Tick.

'Too much hair in your ears,' said Tock.

Tick laughed and Cora smiled.

'You can't laugh your way out of this one,' said the third fairy. He had chin hair that curled meanly every which way.

'How terrible must you be for your own father to banish you,' sneered Glug.

Cora watched as Tick's and Tock's happiness suddenly flew away from them like feathers caught in the wind. Their cheeky smiles disappeared. Then both of the fairies looked down.

Cora stepped forward, anger strengthening her steps.

'These fairies are the kindest fairies I have ever known,' said Cora. She did not mention that they were the *only* fairies she had ever known.

'We shouldn't have come,' Tick whispered to her, pulling on her sleeve.

Cora brushed him away. 'Tick's injured,' she said. 'And needs help. We won't stay long.'

The fairy with plaits looked up at Cora and then over at Tick and Tock. 'You two brought this *creature* to The Hollow.'

Cora thought he was talking about the Jinx and she was about to say that it was her who brought the Jinx to the fairy kingdom, that she was the one to blame and not Tick and Tock, but then the fairy with plaits pointed a small finger in her direction.

Me?! The creature?! thought Cora. 'Hey!'

The fairies glared up at Cora.

'I thought fairies were *supposed* to help one another,' said Cora.

The three fairies in front of her continued to glare.

'I thought people weren't *supposed* to get jinxed,' said the fairy with ear hair down to his knees.

Cora glared back at them. 'Tell us where we can find someone to help him,' Cora said.

'No,' said Glug, folding his arms against his chest.

'Or else,' said Cora.

'Or else what?' asked the fairy, placing his hands on his hips.

'Or else,' said Cora. She hadn't quite thought this through. 'Or else ...' Should she use her powers? 'Or else ... the longer I wait here, the more likely it is the Jinx will find me.' She placed her hands on her hips.

Glug's eyes squinted, but then, with a grimace, the fairy pointed over to one of the huts by the pond. And then he flew angrily away, the other fairies following.

'I never liked Glug,' said Tick.

'Me either,' said Cora with a smile.

Tick and Tock giggled.

'Thank you,' Tock said to Cora.

Cora, Tick and Tock made their way over to the huts by the pond. Cora waited on a chair outside while Tick and Tock went inside.

In no time at all, Tick and Tock emerged from the hut. Tick was flying in the air again. She saw that his wing had a bandage wrapped around the top.

'Are you fixed?' she asked.

'Good as new,' Tick said, flying up into the air in a spin, then he dangled upside down and gave her a wave.

Cora smiled.

Suddenly, there was a series of loud bangs from outside the Fairy Fountain followed by several *POP!s* of magic. They could hear cries and screams. The fairies around them stopped what they were doing.

Cora looked at Tick and Tock. Their eyes were wide.

They'd been found.

Chapter Thirty-Six

Was it the Jinx? The warlock? Cora didn't want to find out.

'We need to get out of here,' said Tick.

They raced out of the Fairy Fountain and entered the Jade City street. The street in front of them was flooded with magical beings. They were all headed towards the city centre.

Confused, Cora, Tick and Tock moved with the crowd until they turned a corner and stopped in their tracks. Cora had come face to face not with a Jinx or a warlock ... but with a giant dragon. She stared up at its red eyes, as it moved freely in the air in front of her. Then it twinkled and Cora realised it wasn't a real dragon. Instead it was made up of small, blinking, coloured lights. It flew above the crowd who oohed and ahhed beneath it.

In front of them, witches, trolls, centaurs, mermaids, hobgoblins and other magical creatures stood near stalls lined up from one end of the street and weaving all the way through Jade City, as far as she could see. People were selling food, clothes, jewellery, hats and all manner of strange and exciting items.

Cora breathed a sigh of relief.

It was a festival.

'Oh,' said Tock. 'Much better than a Jinx!'

'Or a warlock,' said Tick, an excited smile on his face.

The festival reminded Cora of the traders in Urt. Except it was much bigger and … cleaner.

Then there was a crackle of magic and the dragon above her shimmered before disappearing. In its place emerged a giant gold bird. Cora had never seen one like it. It had huge wings, large talons and a sharp beak. It squawked into the air then flew above her before shimmering and disappearing, only to be replaced by a two-headed serpent.

Cora was so busy looking around that she almost didn't hear the sharp *TOOT* from behind her. She looked back to see a group of creatures all dressed in matching blue outfits with pointed hats. They came up to her knees and had long, white beards. Each of them held small, gold instruments in their hands.

'Excuse me,' squeaked the one in front.

'Sorry,' Cora said, quickly stepping out of the way.

'Gnomes,' said Tick as they walked past them and down the street.

'No patience,' said Tock, shaking his head.

Banners and streamers were strung up in the air from stall to stall and building to building.

Then suddenly there were three large bangs, one after another. Cora, Tick and Tock whirled around before looking up to see red fireworks exploding in the blue sky above them.

Then music filled the air. Cora saw that it was coming from the gnomes. They had set up their band on a space of the pavement nearby and were playing a tune that made Cora want to tap her feet.

Happily, Cora, Tick and Tock stepped in time with the festival crowd. They walked past stalls selling soaps that sent shrieking bubbles up into the air, stalls that sold wands that fizzled and sparked, stalls that sold replacement mermaid scales, stalls that sold floating and spinning umbrellas.

As she looked at a spinning umbrella, Cora couldn't help but stare at a man nearby with very beautiful, long, shiny, blond hair.

'Elf,' said Tock by her side.

'Don't worry, we already crossed elf off the list,' said Tick. 'You're not an elf.'

'We think,' added Tock.

'Not enough hair,' said Tick, tilting his head at her.

'I already think I know what I am,' Cora mumbled, remembering Belle the hobgoblin's words. She wished she *was* an elf. They walked past a stall selling different kinds of wigs and watched as a short red wig changed into a long curly one.

'You know what you are?' replied Tock questioningly.

'I'm a Jinx,' she said softly.

There was a pause from the fairies. They stopped flying in the air next to her and stared at her. Then they burst out laughing.

Cora stopped. 'What?' she asked.

Tick was bent over in a fit of giggles. He held onto his stomach.

Tock wiped a tear from his eye.

Cora looked around. What had she said? Some of the people nearby in the crowd around her turned in her direction. Cora glared at the fairies until they stopped laughing.

'Sorry,' said Tock.

'But you can't be a Jinx,' said Tick.

'I can't?' replied Cora. 'But the hobgoblin said …' Cora felt herself go red. She watched as Tick and Tock shook their heads, trying to hold back their laughter.

'You're not big enough,' said Tock.

'Or scary enough,' said Tick.

'And you don't eat people enough,' said Tock.

'So I'm *not* a Jinx?' Cora asked. She suddenly felt lighter.

'Well,' said Tick, 'at least, not *yet*.'

Cora groaned.

'How would that work?' asked Tock. 'If you're jinxed and you are a Jinx?'

Tick stroked his chin in thought. 'Would you … eat yourself?'

Then both of the fairies burst into laughter once more.

Cora rolled her eyes. 'I'm going to look around,' she said. She walked down the festival street, leaving a still-laughing Tick and Tock behind her.

So maybe she wasn't a Jinx. But if she wasn't a Jinx … then what was she? What had the hobgoblin seen inside her? Whatever it was … it had scared her. She hoped Belle was okay.

Cora walked past a stall that sold beetles and another that sold detachable wings, until eventually Cora came to a stall that was empty. She stopped. A woman without any hair stood behind a table with nothing on it. Nobody else was around the stall so Cora walked up to it. At least she thought the stall was empty. As she got closer, she saw some dainty objects glistening in the light. They were crystals. Crystals so clear you could barely see them. They had markings on them but Cora couldn't quite make them out.

The bald woman behind the table looked at Cora interestedly. 'Heart stones,' she said.

Cora reached down and picked up one of the crystals. The marking looked like something she had seen before. She held it closer to her eye, so that it glistened in the sunlight. Then the heart stone nearly fell from her hand when she recognised the marking etched into it. It was the same marking that was burnt into the wooden spellbox she had found in Urt. The one that had summoned the Jinx. The one that had cursed her.

She peered down at it, intrigued.

'Cora,' said Tick and Tock as they flew over to her side. 'Try this!' The pair of them held a bouquet of fairy floss that popped and crackled in their hands.

Hesitantly, Cora grabbed some of the sticky floss and popped it in her mouth. It zapped and buzzed all the way down.

'Fairies,' said a voice from behind them. Cora and the fairies turned around to find a man with pale skin and dark, shaggy, dripping wet hair. His leg was bent

awkwardly and he looked like he could barely stand as he held on tightly to a wooden walking stick. His dark brown eyes flicked from the fairies to Cora.

'I'm Artemis,' he said, breathing heavily. It looked like it had taken him a lot of effort to mutter two words.

Tick and Tock looked the man up and down. He looked familiar. Then Cora remembered where she had seen him. He'd been in line to see King Clang at The Hollow. Cora, Tick and Tock had pushed to the front of the line ahead of him. Then the Jinx …

'I need you to deliver a message,' Artemis said. Then he paused and took a breath. 'I need you to,' he rasped, '... it's of great ... great importance.'

Then the man fainted.

Cora, Tick and Tock peered down at him sprawled on the ground.

'Do you think the message is fainting?' asked Tock.

Chapter Thirty-Seven

'**Q**uickly,' said Cora.

'He's heavy,' said Tock.

'And smelly,' said Tick, wrinkling his nose.

The fairies struggled to keep the man up, holding onto him by his clothes, as they flew through the air. The man bobbed up and down, his hands dragging limply along the ground behind him.

They made their way through the streets away from the festival as fast as they could, which was to say, not very fast. There were people and stalls everywhere. Magical beings looked at them questioningly as they pushed past and Cora did her best to smile and nod politely as if two fairies dragging an unconscious man through the air was a perfectly normal thing.

Carrying his walking stick, Cora led the way through the city, searching for somewhere to stop. 'What about here?' she suggested, pointing down an empty alleyway. There was a rustle from a nearby box and then someone or something let out a giant *BURP*. A strange smell wafted towards them.

Tick and Tock shook their heads.

They moved on.

'Here?' asked Cora motioning to a small park. Then Cora saw something slither through the tall grass. Something big.

Tick and Tock shook their heads.

Eventually they came to a row of homes. One of them had a sign out the front of it that read *VACANT DUE TO PIXIE INFESTATION*.

Cora looked over at Tick and Tock. They nodded, the strain from carrying the man obvious on their faces.

At the back of the house, a rusted door sat ajar. Cora pushed it open and walked inside. Tick and Tock quickly flew in after her. But forgot about the man they were carrying.

BANG!

Artemis's shoulder hit the doorway.

'Oops!' said Tock. 'Tick!'

Artemis groaned.

'Sorry,' said Tick.

'Be careful,' said Cora. She held the door open for the fairies as they pulled the man, this time, more carefully, inside.

The home had all its furniture; couches, cupboards, mirrors, clocks, curtains. It reminded Cora of the houses in Urt that were abandoned in a hurry. Yellow tape stretched from one end of the house to the other. They ducked underneath it.

'Place him here,' said Cora, motioning to the couch in the living room.

Tick and Tock were struggling to keep Artemis up in the air until Tick couldn't carry Artemis any longer and let go of the man's legs just as Tock let go of his arms, and Artemis fell onto the couch with a *THUMP*.

Tick, Tock and Cora looked down at the stranger as he lay still.

Now that they were away from the festival, Cora could see that Artemis's hair and clothes were wet with sweat. His face was red and the leg that was bent in an odd way was soaked with something sticky. Cora touched his leg with a finger and pulled it back to find that the something sticky was blood. He also had red scratches across his hands and neck. They looked like claw marks.

'Everyone,' Artemis muttered. 'All ... nothing ...'

'See if you can find some water,' said Cora. Dot had always said water helped when someone was sick.

With a *POP!*, Tock disappeared.

Cora pulled out the other half of her scarf from her pack and wrapped it around Artemis's injured leg.

Then Artemis started to shake. Cora pulled a curtain from the window and placed it on top of him.

'What do we do, Cora?' Tick asked.

'Can we take him to the Fairy Fountain?' Cora replied.

Tick shook his head. 'The Fountain can only help fairies.'

With a *POP!*, Tock appeared. He held a bucket of water in his hands.

'That's for —' But before Cora could tell Tock what to do with the bucket of water, the fairy threw half of the contents right on top of Artemis. The water splashed all over him.

'Drinking,' finished Cora.

'Oh,' said Tock. 'Oops.'

They waited for the man to wake up, spluttering in shock. But he didn't. Then with a *POP!* of magic, Tock dried him. They waited some more but the man's eyes remained closed. And it wasn't long until Artemis was wet with sweat once more.

'Should we find someone to help him?' Tock asked.

'We don't know what he is yet,' said Tick, looking down at the man. 'What healer do we take him to?'

'He said he needs *our* help,' said Cora, trying to think. She felt a pang of guilt. 'And I remember him. He was at The Hollow waiting to see the king before the Jinx …'

'Do you think this is from the Jinx?' asked Tick.

Cora swallowed. She really hoped not.

They waited. Hours passed and Artemis stayed the same. If anything, he got worse.

'We'll get food,' said Tick. And with two *POP!s*, Tick and Tock disappeared.

Cora looked down at Artemis. He tossed around in his sleep, breathing slow, heavy breaths and murmuring words Cora couldn't quite catch. *What happened to him?* she wondered.

Heat radiated from his skin. Perhaps he had a fever? She thought about checking the way Dot had checked her once before. Gently, Cora reached down towards him and placed a hand on his head. It was hot.

Then suddenly Cora felt a shock go through her entire body. It sparked and sizzled like a bolt of lightning, ricocheting from her toes to her nose. She snatched her hand away and stumbled backwards.

She shook her head. It felt like something was slowly filling her up inside.

Her head spun. She looked over at Artemis. He had stopped stirring and mumbling. His breathing had become softer.

What was that? Whatever it was, it crawled inside her. She felt dizzy. She looked down at her hands. They looked different. Or was that her eye? She could hear herself breathing heavily. Or was that someone else? She felt ... strange.

Just like she had felt before.

Just like after she faced the Jinx at The Hollow ...

Uh-oh.

Chapter Thirty-Eight

There were two *POP!s* and Cora whirled around to find Tick and Tock carrying armfuls of food.

'We found …' began Tock. He stopped when he saw her.

'What happened?'

'What … I … nothing,' said Cora. The vision in her eye was blurry. She tried to blink it away as panic crept through her.

'Cora,' said Tick. The fairies dropped the food they were carrying. Bread and fruit fell to the floor.

'I … I just touched him and …' She looked down at her hands. A feeling squirmed inside her. But it wasn't the same as the one she had felt after The Hollow. Not really. The feeling inside her was different somehow. Instead of a pool of water, it was like wind. A gust of it, swirling around inside her.

Tick and Tock flew in front of her, worried looks on their faces.

Then there was a groan from the floor behind them. They looked over to find Artemis, a hand clutching his head as he struggled to sit up.

'Where …?' he croaked.

Tick and Tock flew over to him and helped him up.

'Here,' said Tock, pushing what was left of the bucket of water towards him. 'It's for drinking.'

Artemis reached down and scooped up a handful of water before gulping it down. Then he splashed some on his face.

Cora squinted over at him. Her vision was blurry but he looked better. Much better. She shook her head and her vision cleared a bit. She could see that Artemis was no longer pale or sweating. His leg was still injured but he no longer looked as ill as he had a few minutes ago. That was quick … wasn't it?

Cora suddenly felt hot. Her head pounded. A dizziness came over her. Flashes of images filled her mind. Feathers floating in the air. A forest at night-time. Screams. Endless screams. She fell to the ground, holding her hands to her head to try to shut out the images.

'Cora?' said Tock, flying over to her.

Tick followed. He looked at Artemis. 'What did you do?'

Artemis stopped, his eyes on Cora. Then he stood up, grabbed his walking stick from the floor and dragged himself over to where she sat. He looked down at her.

Cora felt pain. Sadness. She felt loss. Guilt. It all washed over her in waves. She saw a castle on a hill. She felt cold. She saw a man with long silver hair that glowed. She felt scared.

'I ...' said Cora, unable to put it all into words. It was too much.

Artemis knelt down in front of her.

'Look at me,' he said.

Cora opened her eye. She saw the man's brown eyes peer down at her. They were kind, an understanding in them. Just like Dot's were when she found her.

'Breathe,' Artemis said.

Cora breathed in and then out, focusing on the man's eyes.

'Close your eye. What do you see?'

Cora could see feathers spattered with blood. The castle was empty, smoke billowed from all the windows. The forest was destroyed. An evil laugh echoed in her ears.

'I see a ... castle ... I think,' she said. 'Up high on a hill or a ... a mountain.'

Artemis paused. 'A castle?'

Cora nodded.

'Does it have a large dome made of glass in the centre of it?' Artemis asked.

Cora opened her eye. How did he know that? She nodded. 'And feathers. Everywhere. Blood. Everywhere. A forest. And … a man with silver hair and … white eyes.'

Artemis stood up and stepped back away from her, his eyes wide, his thoughts elsewhere.

Tick and Tock pushed in front of him.

'What is it?' asked Tick.

'Cora, what do you feel?'

'I feel like something is inside,' she said. 'Again.' She had trouble breathing. The feeling was like air this time. It flew around inside her. It was heavy.

Tick and Tock looked at each other.

'You must control it,' said Tick.

'Just like before,' said Tock.

Cora tried to grab the feeling but it moved too quickly. Then she remembered what the hobgoblin had taught her. She stopped trying to fight it. She let the images wash over her. The castle. The forest. The feathers. The man with silver hair and white eyes. She waited. She focused on her breathing like Artemis had told her to do. Then the air got lighter. She let it disappear into her. Then the images in her mind dissolved. And the feeling was gone.

She sat up. Her head slowed its pounding. Her vision became clearer. She looked down at her hands. They looked the same.

Tick and Tock helped her stand.

Artemis stood behind them. He looked over at her as he rested on his walking stick, his eyes assessing.

'Are you okay?' asked Tock.

Cora nodded. Though she wasn't sure.

There was silence in the room.

'Did you feel her?' came Artemis's voice. It was soft. Cora almost didn't hear him. Cora, Tick and Tock looked over at him.

'Who?' asked Cora.

'The princess,' said Artemis. He looked at her.

Cora could see hope in his eyes as he searched her face for an answer.

Cora didn't know what to say. She tried to remember the images.

'You have her magic now, don't you?' Artemis added.

Cora stared at him, not understanding.

'I'm sorry,' he said, shaking his head. 'I've never met someone like you in person. I'd heard stories but I'd never thought …'

'Someone like me?' asked Cora, a sinking feeling in her stomach. She looked at Tick and Tock. They shrugged.

Artemis took a step towards her.

'A syphon.'

Chapter Thirty-Nine

'A what?' exclaimed Cora, confused.

'A syphon,' said Tick and Tock at the same time. There was a *POP!* of magic then they both suddenly held their notepads in their hands. They flicked through the pages.

'That was not on our list,' said Tick looking at his notepad.

'Nope,' said Tock.

A syphon? Cora looked around the room. A tiny flutter of small wings buzzed near her ear. Then something tugged on her hair. Cora swatted it away like a fly.

Artemis stared at her. 'You don't know?'

Cora shook her head. 'Know what?'

'She doesn't know?' Artemis asked Tick and Tock.

'We first thought she was a witch,' said Tick.

'Then we thought she was a giant,' said Tock.

'And for a brief moment we also thought that she could have been a mermaid … but we splashed her with water and nothing happened,' said Tick.

'She is much more than those things,' said Artemis seriously. Artemis looked down at her fiercely.

'Syphons are powerful, magical beings,' he said. 'Like a witch can cast spells, syphons can absorb another's magic just by touching them.'

'I can absorb magic?' Cora repeated. 'What happens to whoever I take it from?' she asked worriedly. She tried to think back to everyone she had ever touched.

'They lose some of their strength,' said Artemis. 'You can absorb some of a power or all of it,' said Artemis. 'You didn't sprout wings when you touched me, for example.'

'You have wings?' Cora asked.

'Syphons are very rare,' said Tock to Cora. 'There aren't many left.'

'If any at all,' added Tick, glancing up at her.

'Because they were hunted for many years,' said Artemis. 'Hunted and killed.'

Cora swallowed. 'Why were they hunted and killed?'

'A well-trained syphon could wield as many as one hundred magical powers. They were a threat to many dangerous people,' said Artemis. 'And a curiosity to others.'

Cora tried to take in everything Artemis was saying.

'The place you saw in your mind, the one with the glass dome on top of a mountain … that is the Avian kingdom,' said Artemis. 'My home.'

'You're an Avian?' asked Tock looking at Artemis admirably.

The man nodded.

'I'm also most likely the last,' he said, glancing down.

'Avians are ancient magical beings that can transform into huge birds,' said Tick in a hushed voice. 'They keep to themselves mostly.'

'I heard they have other powers too,' whispered Tock. 'Like controlling the wind and the rain.'

'Not always,' said Artemis, listening. 'The Princess was able to.'

Cora remembered the giant gold bird made up of lights that flew through the sky at the festival. She looked at the man barely able to stand in front of her and tried to picture him as a bird.

'Our people are ruled by Princess Avette,' Artemis said proudly. Then he stopped, took a sharp breath and closed his eyes. '*Were* ruled.'

'What happened?' Cora asked.

'It was our solstice night,' said Artemis angrily. 'I am … *was* one of the princess's guards. Everyone in the kingdom was celebrating with food and wine. They danced and sang. After the fireworks had ended, the princess said she wasn't feeling well and retired to her bed. Not long after, there was a commotion at the gate. Some of us travelled down the hill to the gate and found a mother and father carrying a sick child. They were begging to be let inside. They said their child was gravely ill and that they needed help. But something didn't feel right. There were no homes for miles. Where had they come from? We found out later that they were just a distraction.' Artemis paused.

Cora saw him grip his walking stick tightly.

'We told them to be on their way but they didn't move. There was a scream from the hilltop and we realised the music had stopped. Then the family, all three of them, transformed in front of our eyes into a giant and an army of gremlins. There were so many of them.

'The giant started to beat down the gate with its massive fists. Some of our people stayed to hold it off and some of us flew back to the kingdom to Princess Avette. But she was gone. There were bloodied footsteps on the ground. Then there was a scream from the forest. Lightning lit up the night sky. It came

from a man with silver hair. We tried to stop him. The princess could only run, her wings had been torn from her.'

Cora remembered the image of the man with silver hair and white eyes. The feathers. The blood.

'Before he could reach the princess, I grabbed her and flew away … but …' Artemis stopped. He took a breath. It was shaky. 'I wasn't fast enough.'

There was silence in the room.

'I'm sorry,' said Cora. 'Is that why you were at The Hollow?'

Artemis nodded. 'King Clang is on The Council. They need to know about what happened. The memories you saw, they were hers,' Artemis said looking up at Cora. 'The princess's.'

'How …?' she said. Artemis's story swirled in her mind.

'When you touched me, you took them,' he said. 'Along with her magic.'

'I didn't mean to,' said Cora honestly. 'I just wanted to see if you had a fever.'

'Princess Avette, before she … she gave me all that she had left. Her magic. Her memories. It gave me strength for a few days. But I couldn't hold onto it. Nobody can hold another person's magic. Nobody … except for syphons.'

He looked at Cora.

All of this was happening too fast. Cora couldn't help but stand up and turn away then walk back and forth in the room. Her thoughts were muddled. But what did this mean? Had she absorbed the princess's magic? Was she a syphon? Was she going to be hunted? Would she ever get back to Urt and find Dot? Cora looked down at her hands. Then she shook her head at Artemis. 'You must be mistaken,' she said to him. Then to herself, 'You have to be.'

'Close that door over there,' Artemis said.

Cora stared at him, uncertain.

'The door. Shut it using her magic,' he said, pointing to the metal door of the house that sat ajar.

Cora stared at it. It wasn't going to work. There was another buzz by her ear and she swatted it away with a hand. Then inside her, she felt something shift. She felt the air around her. She was able to grab it. She felt her hair float up as she pulled the air around her.

'Whoa!' said Tick as he and Tock were blown about in the gust that swirled inside the room. They grabbed onto each other.

Then Cora hurled the air at the door.

And it shut closed with a *BANG*.

Chapter Forty

'That settles it,' said Tock.

'You're definitely a syphon, Cora,' said Tick.

The fairies patted down the little hair that they had on their heads, which had become tousled by the wind. The wind she had conjured up out of thin air.

'I ... I ...' Cora spluttered, breathing heavily. She looked down at herself. She felt it. It had to be true. Relief washed over her. At last she knew what she was. She allowed herself a small smile.

'Where are they?' Cora asked excitedly. 'The other syphons?'

She remembered what Tock had said. *Syphons are very rare.* But that meant there were others, didn't it? Perhaps she could find out where she came from? What her life was before Dot had found her.

Tick shrugged.

'Hidden?' suggested Tock, unsure.

'People will come for her,' said Artemis to the fairies. 'You know that. If they discover what she is …'

Tick and Tock looked at Cora, their faces a mixture of worry and unease. They nodded.

Cora swallowed.

'What if they already are?' Tock asked, hesitantly.

Artemis looked at the fairy questioningly.

'We may or may not be on the run from a Jinx,' said Tock.

'And a warlock,' said Tick.

Artemis stared at them unbelieving.

'It's a long story,' said Tock.

'And the warlock?'

'Archibald is a slightly shorter story,' said Tick.

'Archibald Drake? *The* Archibald Drake? *He's* the warlock that's after her?'

The fairies nodded.

'Cora threw him through a window,' said Tick. 'But he must know what she is.'

'She threw Archibald Drake through a window?' replied Artemis.

'Just a small one,' said Tock.

'Well, a medium-sized one,' said Tick.

But Cora wasn't listening. Her mind swirled with images of an angry Archibald Drake.

Tick and Tock flew over to her.

'Cora, being a syphon … it comes with risks. Grave risks,' said Tock.

'I know. Hunted and killed,' said Cora, repeating Artemis's words. She had been on the run from a Jinx and a warlock. Being hunted wasn't anything new.

'No, not just that,' Tick said, shaking his head. 'The more magic you absorb, the harder it will be to control it. And the harder it will be to stay yourself. Too much magic and …'

'It can tear you apart,' Tock finished, making a pulling motion with his hands.

Cora stared at the fairies. She swallowed the lump that had lodged itself in her throat. She felt the princess's magic inside her. Suddenly she didn't want it. She didn't want to be a syphon. She didn't want any of it. She wished she could go back to when she didn't know what she was. She wished she was at home in Urt with Dot and her cat. Where there was no magic or creatures or warlocks and nobody was torn apart or eaten or hunted.

There was a silence in the room.

Cora shook her head. 'I don't want this.'

Cora put her hands to her temples. Her thoughts were muddled. She tried to think. The more she found out about herself the worse it became. She breathed in. What would Dot do? What would she say? *You're stronger than you think*, were her words. Then Cora remembered. She was strong. She didn't just have the princess's magic … she also had … which meant …

'The Jinx,' she breathed.

Tick and Tock looked over at her.

'That's why the hobgoblin saw the Jinx. Because I … at The Hollow … on the lake. I must have … absorbed some of its magic.'

'You can *eat* people?' Artemis asked.

Cora grimaced. 'What? Ew. No,' she shook her head.

'At least … we hope not,' said Tock warily.

'The *strength* of a Jinx. Just the strength,' said Cora. She was thankful she didn't absorb any other parts of the Jinx.

Cora heard a tiny flutter of small wings near her ear again. What was that? She whipped round, looking around the room. And then as if on instinct she called up the wind around her. It swirled and swirled and then half a dozen pocket-sized, blue creatures flew out from hiding places in the house.

'Pixies!' said Tock.

'I knew I felt something tugging at my ears,' said Tick, holding onto them.

Cora saw Artemis's eyes dart to her wrist, as she

swatted away a pixie. She looked down to see her
bracelet, glistening.

'Ice stone,' Artemis said.

Cora nodded. She remembered the witch's words
at the Black Market of Gwell.

'It's for protection,' said Cora.

'That's it,' said Tick. 'The ice stone!'

Cora and Tock looked at the fairy, confused.

'So you don't tear apart!'

Protection from oneself, the witch had said. The
bracelet *was* protecting her from herself. And if she

was protected … then perhaps … perhaps she was protected for a reason. Someone had given her the bracelet. Who was it? Another syphon? Maybe they wanted her to use her magic.

Suddenly, the ground beneath Cora's feet rumbled. The walls shook and shuddered. She stared at Tick and Tock. Amongst the chaos, amongst everything that had happened over the past few days, she had forgotten all about using the whisper root! She hadn't stayed protected from the Jinx.

'The whisper root,' she said.

Tick and Tock's eyes went wide.

Crashes reverberated outside. There were screams but this time not the festival kind.

The Jinx.

Chapter Forty-One

The walls in the house shuddered. The ceiling shook and crumbled above them. It felt like the Jinx was right on top of them. The pixies flew out from their hiding places, their teeny voices squeaking in alarm. Cora's bracelet tingled on her wrist.

'What is it?' Artemis asked.

'The Jinx,' said Tick, Tock and Cora at the same time.

'It's here? Now?'

'It's a long story,' said Tock.

'Cora may or may not also be cursed,' said Tick. Then he stopped and looked at Tock. 'Hey, perhaps it isn't such a long story.'

Artemis looked at the fairies, not amused.

Cora pictured Jade City in rubble in her mind. She pictured all of the people at the festival running from the shadow creature as it destroyed buildings and homes, searching for her. Just like it had done in Urt.

Just like it had done in The Hollow. It would be the same. But she wasn't the same. She felt the magic inside of her give her strength. It was time she stopped running. Perhaps she *could* do this. Perhaps she was stronger than she thought after all. If she really had magic, if she really was a syphon, then it was time for her to use it. She was sure it would be what Dot would do. She hoped, at least.

'We have to stop it from destroying the city,' Cora said over the loud thundering steps and the rumbling of the house.

'You're going to need some help,' said Artemis, stepping forward.

'But you can barely walk,' said Tock.

Cora shook her head. 'It wants me. Nobody else.'

Artemis straightened, his eyes firm. He looked over at Tick and Tock. 'Promise me that when it's over,' said Artemis, 'and no matter what happens, you will deliver this to The Council.' From out of his pocket, he pulled a wooden box. It was the same as the one Cora had seen the fairies deliver to Archibald at Drake Manor. Except this one was stained with blood.

Cora looked at Tick and Tock. The fairies nodded. With a *POP!* the box disappeared from Artemis's hands and appeared in Tock's.

The house continued to shake, harder now. The Jinx was close. The four of them raced out of the house. Cora led the way with Tick and Tock by her side and Artemis keeping up as best as he could behind them.

When they got to the street outside, they stopped. Grey smoke billowed from buildings throughout Jade City. And then the familiar shadow of the Jinx lumbered around the corner. It was heading straight for them. It let out a large roar before swinging its long arms either side, scraping its claws across the walls of the houses.

Magical beings from all over Jade City ran in the opposite direction. Others threw magic at the creature, trying to stop it in its tracks. A witch sent green, sparkling spells up at it, a group of elves sent arrows from drawn bows but the Jinx just batted them all away with a sweeping, shadowy arm.

Cora stared up at the Jinx. Fear squirmed in her stomach. Her knees began to shake and her palms were sweaty.

'It looks angry,' said Tock.

Cora remembered the last time she had seen the Jinx. She had hit the creature halfway across a lake. *Of course it was angry.*

They watched as the Jinx came to a stop. It had found them. Cora swallowed. What were they going to do? They couldn't just stand there. They needed to do something. Right away. *Think, Cora.* She tried to clear her mind.

Then beside her, Artemis threw his walking stick to the ground. He rolled up his sleeves. Cora could see his arms were covered in dark purple bruises.

'Do you have a plan?' Artemis asked.

Cora nodded. But she didn't have a plan. Not even the slightest of plans. All she could see when she looked up at the Jinx was its burning, yellow eyes. The same ones that had once stopped her in her tracks. But not anymore.

'Okay,' she breathed. 'Here goes nothing.'

She held onto the princess's magic and called up the air around her. She didn't know what she was doing. But the air quickly became a swirling ball of wind that roared in her ears and blew her hair this way and that. Now what? Hesitantly, she pushed the swirling ball of wind at the creature. The Jinx held its claws up against the wind as it flew at him. But the wind wasn't strong enough. The Jinx pushed against it and easily continued to lumber towards them.

Cora let go of the magic, breathing heavily.

Tick and Tock took off. They flew at the Jinx, sending *POP!s* of magic its way. The creature roared at them, its arms stretching out away from the wind to grab them. The fairies tumbled in the air just barely out of reach of the creature's claws.

'You can do this, Cora,' Artemis said beside her. 'Princess Avette said her magic was like flying. Feel the air around you. Float with it like a feather.'

Cora closed her eye. *Focus.* She pictured herself flying, with air around her. She felt light like a feather. She breathed in deeply and then she pushed the wind onto the creature once more. Harder this time. Much harder. Maybe she could lift the Jinx up into the air? And maybe put him somewhere else? Cora tried to shape the air, to push it beneath the Jinx's feet and lift it up off the ground. But the Jinx was heavy. He stumbled with the force of the wind but Cora couldn't lift him up.

Cora opened her eye to see the Jinx try to push back against the roaring wind. But it couldn't. It was forced to stay right where it was. And then it slipped backwards. Cora held the Jinx in place. The shadow creature roared at the wind holding him back. She was doing it.

Cora held on. Keeping the Jinx in place was helping Tick and Tock. They sent more *POP!s* of magic at the Jinx. It roared at them. She tried again to lift up the creature. She gritted her teeth.

Then there was a loud *SNAP* next to her. Cora turned to see Artemis had transformed into a huge gold bird. His feathers glistened like sharp metal in the sun. The bird looked at her with Artemis's eyes. She nodded to him. With a beat of his giant wings, Artemis flew up into the air. He let out a squawk as he soared upwards into the sky and then dived down, straight onto the Jinx, his sharp talons gleaming as they took hold and pulled.

The Jinx roared in pain. It looked up and used both of its arms to grab Artemis and yank the bird off. But Artemis was too fast. He flew up and soared out of the way of the Jinx's long arms just in time. Tick and Tock continued throwing magic at the creature. The Jinx toppled backwards, falling to the ground. Then it heaved itself to its feet.

Cora felt her magic weakening. She couldn't hold onto the wind much longer. She let go of the magic. Breathing heavily, she fell to her knees. Dizziness clouded her mind. She shook her head and tried to ignore it.

She watched as the Jinx dove at Tick and Tock. Cora winced as it let out another roar, blowing Tick and Tock over in the air.

Cora caught her breath. She needed to help them. Perhaps she could throw something? Like she had done at the lake? She searched around her for something she could use. Lying on the ground next to her was Artemis's walking stick.

Cora picked up the walking stick and looked for the strength of the Jinx inside her. She found it. Then she threw the stick as hard as she could in the direction of the Jinx. She used the wind around it to push it through the air like a spear. It shot towards the creature but the Jinx turned at the last minute and the walking stick went soaring right past him and through a nearby window. The Jinx didn't even flinch.

Come on, Cora, she said angrily to herself.

Artemis dove at the Jinx again but the creature moved out of the way. Sparks of magic flew up at the Jinx from the ground. Cora looked around and saw the magical beings of Jade City helping them against the Jinx.

The creature roared down at them in anger. Then with one giant hand the Jinx jumped up and grabbed Tock, plucking him out of the air. The fairy was trapped in the creature's claws.

'No!' Cora cried.

The Jinx let out a roar and then lifting up its arm, it dangled Tock from two of its claws. The Jinx opened its mouth wide and lowered its arm. It was going to *eat* Tock!

Chapter Forty-Two

Cora ran. She ran towards the Jinx as fast as she could. She could only watch, her heart beating fast and her eyes wide, as Tock was lowered towards the Jinx's mouth. From above, she saw Tick fly down to the Jinx, towards his brother but with its other hand, the Jinx swatted the fairy away. Tick went flying up into the air.

'Tick!'

She raced towards them. When she got closer, she could see Tock still in the Jinx's clenched hand. He tried to squirm out of the creature's grasp. 'Stop!' Cora cried as she ran. 'Don't! I'm here!' But she was too far from them, the Jinx couldn't hear her.

The Jinx's arm got lower and lower. Tock tried to scramble away from the gaping black hole that was the Jinx's mouth.

Cora gritted her teeth. She felt the magic inside her. She grabbed the princess's magic. She grabbed the air. And used it around her to push herself faster towards them.

Don't!

Then the Jinx stopped, Tock inches from its mouth. The Jinx turned in her direction and looked down at her.

Could the Jinx … did he *hear* her? She was close enough to smell the shadow creature now. She looked up and into the sky. It was time all of this came to an end.

'It's me you want!' she yelled. She continued running at full speed. The air around her pushed her forward. Then grabbing the strength of the Jinx she had inside, she reached the Jinx's leg and pushed as hard as she could.

'Argh!' she cried.

The Jinx's leg flew up and backwards into the air, then it fell, crashing down onto a building behind it. A dusty plume of smoke went up into the air and the ground shook beneath Cora. She waited for the Jinx to get up. But it stayed down. She saw Artemis fly over to it and dive into the grey smoke to find Tock.

Cora looked around. Some of the magical beings nearby were watching from hiding places. Others were breathing heavily from using their magic against the Jinx. She saw the smoke and the buildings and homes around her destroyed.

Breathing heavily, Cora waited for Artemis and Tock to emerge. She felt the strength still under her skin. Then suddenly Cora felt something grab her by the throat. Its grasp became tighter and tighter until

she couldn't breathe. She looked around, wide-eyed but she couldn't see anybody. She was lifted up off the ground, her feet dangling beneath her. She clutched at her neck. Her vision became blurry. Then someone slowly spun her around in the air.

Standing in the street behind her, his coat and dark hair trailing in the wind, was Archibald Drake. The warlock.

Cora heard a squawk in the air followed by quick *POP!s* of magic. She watched silently as Artemis, Tick and Tock came into view, diving towards the warlock.

No.

Archibald looked up, then holding up one of his hands, he motioned to the huge gold bird and suddenly Artemis hung suspended in the air, just like Tick and Tock had been in the witch's shop. Then Archibald turned his hand and Artemis twisted and turned in the air.

'Artemis!' she rasped.

He let out a loud squawk of pain.

Then Tick and Tock sent sparks of magic at the warlock. One of them hit Archibald in the shoulder and he dropped the hand that was holding her throat.

Cora fell to the ground, gasping in all the air she could.

Archibald curled up his hand and moved it up

and then down, sending Artemis flying upwards and then straight down, right through the roof of a home nearby.

'No!' she croaked.

Cora waited for Artemis to emerge, soaring up into the sky from where he lay slumped amongst broken beams. But he didn't.

Tick and Tock sent more *POP!s* of magic at the warlock from the air. Archibald deflected them, sending the sparks of magic back at the fairies. Tick and Tock tried to fly out of the way in time but they weren't fast enough. The sparks of magic hit them.

'Tick! Tock!' Cora yelled.

The fairies tumbled out of the sky. They fell down, down, down in what seemed like slow motion. Then Tick and Tock hit the ground, rolling with a bounce to a stop. Unmoving.

Cora stared at her friends. She willed them to get up. To smile and brush it off. But they lay still.

Cora turned around to find Archibald, his dark eyes on her and a smile on his worn face. An anger, which Cora had never felt before, bubbled and popped beneath her skin like a boiling stew. It was more than she had ever felt before. More than she knew she could ever feel. Was it the princess? Was it the Jinx?

She thought about the scavengers in Urt. The ones who had taken the shoe polish from her. She thought about what she would have said to them if she'd had the courage. And as she glared at the warlock, she only knew one thing.

You've messed with the wrong girl.

Chapter Forty-Three

'**D**o you have any idea the power I wield?' the warlock called out to her. 'For sixteen years I was Warlock of the Seven.'

Cora wasn't listening. She focused on the princess's power. She focused on the Jinx's strength. She combined them in her mind. She felt her skin sting as her fists clenched shut by her waist.

'And then a *girl* with *one eye* throws *me* through a window,' the warlock growled. 'For everyone in the Black Market to see.'

The warlock lifted a finger and Cora felt something run across her arm. She looked down to see a small cut. A terrible fury rolled around inside her. It became stronger and stronger with every word the warlock uttered.

'Your power,' he said, pointing to her scar. 'It won't last.' He took a step forward towards her. 'I felt it when I first saw you. You can't control it.'

Cora ignored him. She focused on what she was doing. Both magics took a hold of her. She felt stronger. More powerful than she had felt before.

'I wasn't prepared for you,' he said. 'But I am now.' The warlock held his hands out at either side of him as he continued walking towards her. Black sparks crackled at the tips of his fingers.

Cora watched as a malicious grin spread across Archibald's face. *He's playing with me.* Just like Scratch used to do with the mice he would find behind the wall. *But why?*

'It's going to eat you alive,' said the warlock. 'You're pathetic. A nobody. You'll never be able to keep absorbing magic.'

Another cut sliced across her leg. She ignored it. She held onto the princess's magic tightly. The sky above her darkened with rolling grey clouds. White rage thundered through her.

'Well,' the warlock spat, 'show me what you can do!' The warlock pointed at her and Cora felt another cut slice across her leg. She didn't look down this time. Artemis's words flashed through her mind, *People will come for her … if they discover what she is.*

'Can't you do it because your flying friends aren't around to help you anymore?' Archibald goaded. Pointing, the warlock sent a cut across her cheek. Cora breathed in. Cora remained still, trying to control the magic inside her. She could do it. She could hold on —

'Fairies are the dirt beneath our feet,' sneered the warlock.

And with a *SNAP*, Cora's anger exploded like lightning. She closed her eye and called up the air around her. Along with everything she had left. All of it. Every pain and worry she had. Dot. Scratch. Urt. Tick. Tock. Artemis. Their faces flashed in her mind. Everything she had ever felt, she rolled it all into one.

Suddenly the air around her transformed into a whirling, booming gale. Her hair flew out of its ribbon as she focused on the magic inside her.

Archibald glanced up at the darkened sky, then around them at the roaring wind. Then he laughed. 'Is that it?! Is that all you can do?! You don't scare me, girl.'

Cora opened her eye and stared daggers at the warlock.

'You don't scare me either,' she said.

Then with all the strength she had left, Cora sent the wind towards the warlock. She grabbed him, plucking him off the ground and pulled him towards her so fast that she almost didn't see him. The warlock struggled against the wind, reaching out both hands to grab her. But Cora held him back. She pushed him down towards the ground so that she could look him in the eyes. He writhed in front of her, breaking free from her hold. Cora shoved him back, using the strength of the Jinx but the warlock held up his hands and her strength bounced away from him like a pebble ricocheting against stone.

Cora swallowed. She felt herself weakening. Archibald had started to get to his feet. He was too powerful. What could she do? There was only one thing left she could think of. But could she do it? She had done it before. Although, not on purpose.

Before Archibald could stand up straight, Cora quickly put her hand over the warlock's face.

'What are you doing,' he spluttered.

Cora felt the familiar shock shoot through her entire body. It sizzled from her toes to her nose. She closed her eye and let it seep into her, filling her up with energy. When the feeling faded away, she let go of him.

The warlock dropped to the ground in front of her.

Cora stepped back. Her head pounded with pain. Her vision was blurred around the edges. Her legs were wobbly beneath her. The wind and dark clouds slowly disappeared.

In front of her, the warlock clambered angrily to his feet. 'You can't,' he said. 'You're not strong enough.' He stumbled, holding his hand to his face where she had touched him. 'I'm too powerful for you to withstand!'

Cora straightened and stared back at him. Then she held out her hands either side of her. Black sparks crackled at the tips of her fingers.

The warlock's eyes widened.

Then Cora noticed a dark shadow behind the warlock. It was the Jinx. It must have removed itself from the building and was now lumbering towards them.

Archibald's face was twisted with rage. He was so consumed with anger he didn't even seem to feel the ground shaking beneath their feet. Instead, he held his hands up in the air, his eyes on her wrist. Then Cora felt the skin on her arm become hot like it was placed over a fire. She lifted up her arm and watched wide-eyed as her bracelet fell apart like soft snow, melting off her wrist to the ground.

'Now there's nothing to protect you,' he snarled, blood dripping down from his nose.

Then Archibald lifted Cora up off the ground with his magic. Her throat began to tighten again. She could see that the Jinx was close. She didn't have much time. She searched inside herself. She found the warlock's power. It sparked and fizzed like electricity.

She let it become part of her, flowing through her like a current. Then she searched for what she was looking for. And found it. Using her hands, she broke free of the warlock's hold on her and dropped to the ground.

Sucking in air, Cora stood up and with both of her hands she held the warlock in place, lifting him up into the air, just like he had done to her.

Before the warlock could do anything, the Jinx was on them. From right above the warlock, the creature looked down, and then with one gigantic swipe, it swatted the warlock out of its path.

With a cry, Archibald Drake went flying up into the air like a doll before falling back down streets away, somewhere in Jade City. Cora hoped it was the last they would see of Archibald Drake.

She held onto the warlock's magic as the Jinx looked down at her. She braced herself. Was it her turn next?

Then slowly, the Jinx bent down so that it was crouched on one knee. Its head was now at her height and the creature peered at her with interest.

Cora tried to still her heartbeat as she stared into the Jinx's glowing, yellow eyes. *This is it*, she thought. The thick smell of ash and smoke filled the air. From up close, she could see the shadows that made up the Jinx. They floated around her like thin, black curtains.

Then the Jinx bent towards her and its two big nostrils sniffed the air around her.

Cora closed her eye.

She waited. What was taking so long?

Cora opened her eye to see the Jinx still in front of her. It hadn't moved an inch. She looked down at herself. It definitely hadn't eaten her. Why hadn't it eaten her?

Then the Jinx extended a hand towards her.

Cora thought it was about to grab her but it stopped and instead touched her gently on the forehead. Its hand felt cool against her skin. Cora shuddered.

Then the Jinx let go and placed the same hand on its own forehead.

Cora didn't understand what it was doing.

The Jinx stood up. The ground shook as it got to its feet. The creature stared down at Cora and then with a shudder, its shadows floated up into the air and the Jinx disappeared.

Chapter Forty-Four

Cora suddenly felt a wave of exhaustion. She collapsed onto the ground and sat with her head in her hands. What had the Jinx done? She still felt its strength inside her. But she also felt lighter, somehow. She looked around her. Most of the Jade City street was destroyed. The homes and buildings lay in crumbled parts.

Crud.

There was movement in the rubble nearby. Cora turned to find Artemis. No longer a bird, he hobbled over to her. His leg looked worse than before. She probably shouldn't have thrown his walking stick into a building.

'Are you alright?' Cora asked. 'Your walking stick is, uh,' she pointed vaguely to one of the buildings in the distance.

Artemis nodded. 'What happened?' he asked, a hand on his head.

'I'm not entirely sure,' Cora said honestly.

She looked around the street. There was no sign of Tick or Tock.

'Have you seen …?' she began and then she heard the flutter of wings.

From a bit further down the street, the fairies flew over to them. Relief washed over Cora as she watched Tick and Tock fly and land on the ground beside her with a *THUD*.

'You're both okay,' said Cora happily. She couldn't shake the memory of the fairies still and unmoving on the street.

Then the fairies collapsed on their backs, breathing in and out heavily.

'That …' breathed Tick.

'… was close,' groaned Tock.

Cora looked the fairies over carefully. They were covered in scratches and bruises. Tock's nose was bent at an odd angle and his face was bruised with blotches of purple. And when Tick smiled up at her, Cora thought that the fairy might be missing a tooth or two.

'What did we miss?' asked Tick.

The fairies and Artemis glanced over at Cora.

She paused. Cora wasn't sure what to tell them.

'Did you defeat the Jinx?' asked Tock with a smile.

'Not exactly,' said Cora. She thought about the Jinx and how it had just disappeared. *Why didn't it eat me?* she wondered.

'And Drake?' asked Tick.

Perhaps it was better to show them? Cora held out her hands either side of her. Black sparks flickered from her fingertips.

Tick and Tock sat up, their eyes wide.

'You …' said Tick

'Warlock magic?' finished Tock.

Cora nodded.

'Cora, warlock magic, it's …' said Tock.

'Dark magic,' finished Tick.

'I know,' Cora said, remembering what they had told her about Archibald. 'But it was the only way to stop him. It was the only way to … protect everyone.' At least, that's what she thought at the time.

Tick and Tock looked at each other.

'You must be careful with it,' said Tock.

'What about the Jinx?' Tick asked.

'It didn't try to eat me,' she said.

The fairies raised their eyebrows at her.

'It could have. I was right there,' Cora said. 'But it just touched me. And then … it disappeared.'

'It didn't eat you?' asked Tick.

'Not even a nibble?' added Tock.

Cora shook her head.

'The curse,' said Artemis.

Cora and the fairies looked over at him.

'It must have freed you from it,' Artemis said.

'Do you feel any diapers?' Tick asked.

'Different,' corrected Tock.

'Do you feel any different?' Tick repeated.

'I … I don't know,' Cora said. She closed her eye and searched. She felt a little different but she thought that was the warlock magic. But maybe it could be … She opened her eye and looked at Tick and Tock. 'A little?'

The fairies shrugged.

'It's … over,' said Cora, unbelieving. 'It's really over,' she looked at Artemis then back at the fairies. They smiled at her.

Cora stood up and spun around on the spot. She felt a weight tumble from her shoulders and hit the ground. *It's over. The curse is lifted.*

Cora looked out and saw that some of the magical beings of Jade City had started to help repair the damaged street, the sound of *POP!s* of magic in the air.

Tick waved to them.

'Do you think we will be allowed back to Jade City?' Tock asked looking around at the mess they had made.

'Probably not,' said Tick.

There was silence amongst them.

'What now?' Cora asked.

'We were thinking of having a nap,' said Tick.

'For five days,' said Tock.

Cora smiled. Then she looked over at Artemis. 'Thank you,' she said. 'For all of your help.'

Artemis nodded.

'We will deliver your message to King Clang,' said Tock.

'We will tell him about the silver-haired man,' said Tick.

'And what happened to the princess,' added Cora.

'Thank you,' said Artemis.

'Where will you go?' Cora asked. As she looked around, she couldn't help but think the same thing about herself.

'Home,' said Artemis. 'The kingdom is destroyed but maybe some of my kind were able to escape the silver-haired man.'

Cora thought on Artemis's words. *Home.* She always thought Urt was her home ... but perhaps she had another home somewhere. The one she couldn't remember.

'If you ever need me,' Artemis said, 'just send word.'

Cora and the fairies nodded.

And then with a *SNAP*, Artemis transformed into a great golden bird. He bent his head down in a bow before taking off in flight, beating his great wings into the air.

The three of them watched as Artemis flew up and over the evening sky of Jade City.

Then Tick sighed. 'I wish we had wings like that.'

Chapter Forty-Five

*C*ora, Tick and Tock helped the magical beings of Jade City repair the destruction left behind by the Jinx. Magic sparks zipped in the air as they put bricks back, smoothed cracks in the streets, mended roofs and windows. Cora helped an ogre lift up a slanted house and Tick and Tock scooped up debris with the help of a group of diligent gnomes.

When the evening sky turned into night, Cora and the fairies threw themselves down on the ground, well and truly exhausted. The street was ramshackle and not quite right — Cora spotted an upside-down roof on a house nearby — but it was close.

As they sat, Cora could hear the music from the Jade City festival begin again in the distance. She smiled. She felt lighter, the curse no longer clinging to her like a shadow. She was free. But beneath her relief swam a sinking feeling in her stomach. She glanced down at her wrist and saw it bare. She was no longer protected by her bracelet. *The more magic you absorb, the harder it will be to control it*, Tick's words rang in her mind. And Tock's, *It can tear you apart.* She swallowed and quickly pulled her jacket sleeve down over her wrist.

'Cora?' said Tock.

'Huh?' she said, her mind elsewhere. She looked back at the fairies.

'Are you alright?' Tock asked.

Cora nodded.

'I suppose you're going to go back home?' asked Tick after a while. 'To Urt.'

Home. Cora thought about that word again.

'To find your Dot and Scrap?' added Tock.

'Scratch,' Cora corrected with a smile. She wanted to go back to Urt. To find Dot and Scratch. She wanted to see them again, more than anything. But something inside her was pulling her elsewhere. *Home.* She thought about her bracelet again. Who had given it to her? If there were other syphons, then where were they? Maybe she could find them. Her heart quickened at the thought. She didn't know what world she belonged to. But maybe she could find out.

'Yes, I'd like to go home,' Cora said.

Tick nodded sadly. He wiped his nose on his sleeve.

Tock rubbed one of his eyes with his shirt.

'But I don't think Urt is home anymore,' she said. 'So I think I might stick with you two until I find it, if that's okay?'

The fairies looked at Cora, large grins spread across their faces. Then they flew at her, barrelling into her with hugs. She hugged them back.

Cora was happy. So happy that she ignored the faint crackle of warlock magic that sizzled and sparked strangely beneath her skin.

When they let go of Cora, Tick and Tock flew upwards, twirling and somersaulting happily in the air.

'I think our work here is done,' said Tick proudly.

'To the Hollow!' said Tock.

'Are you sure we'll be allowed back in?' Cora asked.

'Banished! Schmanished!' said Tick.

Cora laughed.

'And without that pesky Jinx chasing us, we can travel however we please,' said Tock.

Cora remembered the travel sickness she felt when they arrived at Drake Manor. 'Oh no.'

'Hold onto your stomach!' said Tock.

Then Tick and Tock flew down towards her and with a final *POP!* of magic, Cora and the fairies disappeared from Jade City, a soft echo of laughter in the air.

to be continued . . .

Rebecca McRitchie would love to tell you that she was raised by wolves in the depths of a snow-laden forest until she stumbled upon and saved a village from the fiery peril of a disgruntled dragon.

But, truthfully, she works as a children's book editor and lives in Sydney.

Whimsy and Woe and the sequel, *Whimsy and Woe: The Final Act*, were her first fiction titles, followed by the Jinxed! series.

Sharon O'Connor is a freelance illustrator who lives in Melbourne with her husband and triplet sons.

After graduating from R.M.I.T. Graphic Design, she has spent many years designing and illustrating in publishing, textiles and packaging with a particular love of charater design. In her spare time she likes to paint, bake, hang out with animals and take lots of photos.

WHIMSY AND WOE

by Rebecca McRitchie
illustrated by Sonia Kretschmar

After being abandoned by their thespian parents, Whimsy and Woe Mordaunt are left in the care of their austere Aunt Apoline.

Forced to work in Apoline's boarding house, slaving at the beck and call of outlandish and demanding guests, and sharpening the thorns of every plant in the poisonous plant garden, Whimsy and Woe lose all hope that their parents will ever return. Until one day, quite by accident, the siblings stumble upon a half-charred letter that sets them on a course to freedom and finding their parents.

'Adventurous and outlandish, *Whimsy and Woe*
will hook kids in from the first page'
Books+Publishing, ★★★★

WHIMSY AND WOE: THE FINAL ACT

by Rebecca McRitchie
illustrated by Sonia Kretschmar

As a blazing inferno rages through Whitby City, Whimsy and Woe Mordaunt see their last clue go up in flames and their journey to find their parents has seemingly come to a fiery end. That is until the siblings spot a very familiar man in the crowd …

In the final act to this dramatic tale, Whimsy and Woe must escape villainous thieves, travel beneath a desert, climb the Mountainous Mountains and perform a death-defying trapeze act in the Benton Brothers Circus … all before going undercover at the annual Thespian Society Masquerade Ball.

Can they stop The Purple Puppeteer's evil plans in time and rescue their parents? Or will The Purple Puppeteer pull their family's strings forever?